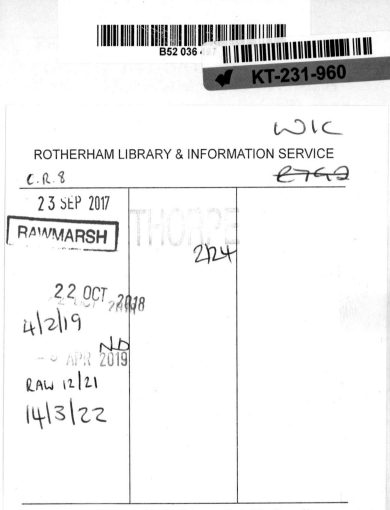

THE MISSING ATTORNEY

The lone survivor of a car accident during a winter snowstorm, Hal Watson is left stranded far from home. He has just witnessed the gruesome murder of his daughter, Marilyn — but will he be rescued in time to prevent a miscarriage of justice? Attorney Gail Brevard and her colleagues are dismayed when Marilyn's fiancé, Damon Powell, is accused of the crime. Gail had successfully defended Damon when he was charged with murder five years earlier. Is this a copycat killing, or is there a serial killer on the loose?

Books by Mary Wickizer Burgess
in the Linford Mystery Library:

THE PURPLE GLOVE MURDERS
HANGOVER HILL

with Ana R. Morlan:
GRAVE WATERS

MARY WICKIZER BURGESS

THE MISSING ATTORNEY

Complete and Unabridged

LINFORD
Leicester

First published in Great Britain

First Linford Edition
published 2017

A catalogue record for this book is available
from the British Library.

ISBN 978–1–4448–3274–7

Published by
F. A. Thorpe (Publishing)
Anstey, Leicestershire

Set by Words & Graphics Ltd.
Anstey, Leicestershire
Printed and bound in Great Britain by
T. J. International Ltd., Padstow, Cornwall

This book is printed on acid-free paper

Dedicated to the Memory of
Judge Russell Alger Wickizer
(1899–1966)
And, as always, to Michael

1

The black sedan bounced along the rough gravel fire road leading deeper and deeper into the wooded hills. From time to time the driver glanced nervously into the rearview mirror, trying to gauge the body language of the hooded individual in the back seat.

'How much further? This road looks like it's about to run out.'

'Shut up and keep driving until I tell you to stop.'

The steely nose of a half-concealed revolver was pointed directly at the back of the driver's head.

Peering through the gathering dusk, the driver could see the road veering off sharply to the right, just above a deep gorge hidden by a thick bramble of undergrowth and close-bound trees. All save the firs were now denuded of their leaves in anticipation of the winter to come.

The road narrowed even further, and

the ruts grew deeper. The driver struggled to compensate against the car's steering mechanism, then lost the battle.

'What are you doing?' a hoarse shout erupted from the back seat.

But it was too late.

The car slid sideways in the damp gravel and poked its nose over the brink. In spite of a last valiant effort by the driver to regain control, first the hood, then the body of the car careened down the side of the abyss into the darkness below. One wheel continued to spin crazily for a moment or two ... then silence.

* * *

The driver gradually regained consciousness. At first he believed he was at home in his own bed, in that dreamless state just before waking when one is safe and all is well. His soul longed to linger in that split second before the harsh reality of daylight intruded on shadowed eyelids.

It was almost comfortable, lying to one side like this, belly and shoulder still harnessed in. It seemed restful and still ... and yet … the awareness that something was terribly wrong began to sink in.

At last, struggling to an upright position, he turned and glanced into the back seat. The body of his unwanted passenger was twisted, the head cocked back in an unnatural position. The gun had fallen harmlessly to one side. There was no sound of breathing, and the driver could detect no rise and fall of the chest to indicate there was still respiration.

Gradually maneuvering his girth, the driver examined the seat-belt fastener, and after a few manipulations it clicked open easily. Good! Now to get free of the car.

The automobile had come to rest against the driver's door, which was caved in from the impact and would not open. Gingerly sliding across the gearbox to the passenger's side of the front seat, the driver tried the door. It opened a crack, but was snug up against a stout fir limb. He laid back and began kicking at it, trying to muster all possible strength.

Finally, after several minutes of concentrated effort, first there was a cracking sound, then the whole door and tree branch

3

gave way. There was just enough room to slide out, feet first, onto solid ground.

Before exiting, the driver cautiously reached over the back seat and grabbed for the gun lying just out of reach of the inert passenger's hand. *Can't be too careful*, he thought, easing out through the passenger door onto the uneven leaf-carpeted dirt. *My captor might not be dead. I don't know exactly where I am … or how long it will take to get out of here.*

I've got the advantage now, and I intend to keep it until I'm safe.

2

Gail Brevard sat back from the brief she was reviewing, hit Save, and stretched. She reached for a bowl of hard candies and popped one in her mouth, then rose and walked over to the window of her comfortable office suite, which was situated in an upper corner of the firm of Osterlitz and Brevard located on Main Street in the bustling town of Cathcart. The late-afternoon sky was filled with tell-tale yellowish-gray clouds threatening rain.

Or snow, she thought, shivering slightly and wrapping her arms around her upper body. *Erle would be thrilled if it snows*. It had been a while since she had planned an outing with her brother. Maybe she could carve enough time out of her schedule to drive to their favorite sledding spot and spend an afternoon rollicking in the snow. Then back to town for hot chocolate before a roaring fire.

Her mother could certainly use the break.

Which led her down a tricky path. Alberta Norris was a strong woman, both by nature and by need. When Gail's younger brother was born, her parents were ecstatic. Here was the son and heir, destined to step into his father's shoes when the time came, and take over the helm of the family law firm. Young Erle Stanley Norris was a beautiful infant, with thick dark curly hair and big bright blue eyes. People would stop Alberta in the street to coo at the baby as she trundled him about town, shopping and running errands.

But as time went by, Erle didn't change. He grew all right physically, as expected, into a handsome, sturdy young toddler. But the words were slow in coming, and he had great difficulty in learning even basic skills. His attention span was short, and the temper outbursts were frequent, including frightening episodes of head-banging and frothing at the mouth.

Joseph and Alberta Norris beat a steady path back and forth to the doctors that first year, and finally got the diagnosis everyone had dreaded. Erle was developmentally disabled. He would probably not advance mentally beyond the age of five or six. And he would need supervision and oversight for the rest of his natural life. Erle Stanley Norris would never be able to live on his own — and he most certainly would never practice law.

Joe Norris took action. His attention turned to Gail, his eldest child, and he began a program of intense training and education that would prepare her for law school and, eventually, taking over his practice. Gail had thrived on all that attention, and had responded with enthusiasm. She took Latin, as well as Spanish and French, and she doubled up on classes in history, sociology and English. She was president of the debating team in high school, and served as a representative to the state junior legislature. She graduated with honors, and began sifting through the many university offers that came her way.

And all the while there was Erle. Big, soft, gurgling Erle. And Alberta, in spite of the therapists' recommendations to institutionalize him, stayed home and took care of him. She gave over her life to her son, and Joe Norris gradually faded into

7

the background. Yes, they still went places together and kept up the pretense of a social life. But for all intents and purposes, Alberta's attention was focused solidly on Erle ... and Joe's was on Gail. Somehow they made it work. But it had been difficult.

Now, in spite of her reluctance to admit it, Gail was certain she had detected the tell-tale signs of fatigue and aging in her mother. Erle, physically an adult, could be a handful, particularly when things didn't go his way. He didn't throw tantrums as often these days, but he could be sullen and even menacing if crossed.

When Gail worried aloud about the situation, Connie, her partner in all things, would stop her, saying in his no-nonsense way, 'For God's sake, Gail, let's just move them in here ... or sell this place and get a bigger one ... or move your mother into assisted living and bring Erle here ... something, anything to ease your mind.' But Gail still wasn't ready to confront Alberta about her fears. So things remained in limbo.

Reluctantly, and with a sigh, she returned to the computer and began reviewing again where she had left off. The case in which she was immersed was complicated, and took her utmost attention; yet she felt restless, almost bored somehow, by the mundane task at hand. She shook her head, unwilling to succumb to the temptation to wrap it up for the day. There were still a few hours left in which she could make progress.

Just then, she heard a commotion in the outer office. Loud voices erupted, punctuated by the door to the inner sanctum opening abruptly.

'Wait a moment, sir. Do you have an appointment? You can't just — '

'I can do anything I like, miss,' was the harsh response.

Gail's intercom crackled, and Melanie the receptionist, high-pitched voice trembling, pleaded: 'Ms. Brevard, *please* come out at once. There is someone — '

She stood up as her door burst open. A familiar face greeted her. 'Officer Hudson. What are you doing here?'

'*Detective* Hudson to you, Counselor. I'm here on business.'

'What business?' An icy finger of apprehension traced its way across her shoulders, but she stood firm and held the policeman's eyes.

'Where is Damon Powell? I have business with him.'

'Damon? What on earth are you talking about? I don't know if he's in today or not. He sometimes attends classes this time of day.'

'I have a warrant for his arrest.'

'His arrest? You must be mistaken. He's been a model citizen since … since his trial. You must know that. He's been interning with us, and working part-time for Hugo for the past several years, and attending college.' She paused.

'In any case, I'm his attorney, and whatever business you have with Damon, you must take it up with me. Where's the warrant?'

'I'll take the question of his attorney up with Mr. Powell himself, if you don't mind. He can decide if he needs an attorney after I've read him his rights. Now where is he?'

Gail took a moment to gather her thoughts, taking in the hot-headed Charlie Hudson, dressed today in a navy-blue suit and tie, and backed up by several burly uniformed officers milling about in the hallway. She wondered when he had been promoted, and why. Hudson was very much a loose cannon, a fact well-known by the legal community. He must have done a lot of apple-polishing to get in line for detective.

'Very well,' she said. 'Let's go over to Hugo's office and see if he knows where Mr. Powell is working today, or if he's attending classes. Follow me.'

Brushing past the glowering detective, Gail headed toward the back of the building where Hugo Goldthwaite maintained his offices. The Goldthwaite Detective Agency was an independent contractor, and had many outside clients in Cathcart. But the proprietor, Hugo Goldthwaite, Jr., had a special arrangement and connection with Gail and her partner Conrad 'Connie' Osterlitz. His father, Hugo, Sr., now retired, had founded the firm years earlier. Father and son had worked on many cases with Gail and Connie, including the Damon Powell murder trial five years earlier. The detective agency leased its offices within the law firm as a matter of convenience to both, since they frequently worked cases together.

Gail considered Hugo her right-hand man in tricky circumstances. He had saved the day for them many times — and her life as well, on at least one occasion. He was a tried and true colleague and friend, and he had taken on Damon and given him a job when it would have been difficult for the young man to find employment anywhere else. The position had worked out to everyone's satisfaction, and now Damon was attending law school and interning for Gail in his spare time, with an eye to joining the firm after he passed the bar. Damon Powell had made a complete turnaround in his life, and was well on his way to a successful and meaningful career.

Hugo's suite door was ajar, and glancing inside, Gail saw several of his operatives seated at a long work table near the window, going over files and comparing notes. Leading Hudson through, she found Hugo working at the computer on his paper-strewn desk.

'Oh, hi, Gail.' He paused, taking in the detective and his back-up team. 'What's up?'

'Hugo, do you know what Damon's

schedule is today? Off — *Detective* Hudson needs to speak with him.' She emphasized the word 'Detective' with a raised eyebrow in Hudson's direction.

'Well, he came in this morning. I don't think he had any classes today, and he came back from lunch a while ago. Last time I saw him he was in the library, checking out some back cases for me. Shall I ... ?' He started to get to his feet, but Gail waved him back.

'That's all right; we'll find him. Thanks, Hugo. And would you see if Connie's back from court yet? We may need his assistance here.' She looked directly into Hugo's eyes and shook her head slightly.

Hugo nodded. 'Will do, Gail. And let me know if you need anything else.' He gazed meaningfully at the police presence and reached for his phone. 'I'll see if I can scare up Connie,' he added, punching in a speed-dial number.

Gail waded back through the uniformed cops and led them all back down the hall toward the law library and conference room at the other end of the floor. Her mind was whirling as she went over the possibilities in her mind. What on earth could they want with Damon? She had to protect him, if at all possible, from any kind of railroading plot. There were still quite a few people in Cathcart who believed her client had escaped the earlier murder charges in some illegal way. And unfortunately, that earlier murder had never been solved. After more than five years, it was now considered a cold case. And public opinion died hard.

The whole affair had been tough on Damon, who had been little more than a snot-nosed kid at the time, trying to act as tough as he could. But Gail gave him credit for the fact that after the affair was settled in his favor, he had held his head high and moved on with his life as best he could. He ignored all the people who talked behind his back, and was now expending every effort to make his future count for something positive. Although the rule of double jeopardy would prevent Damon from being tried for the original murder again, it would be extremely difficult to get him a fair trial for any new charges.

And if Damon *hadn't* committed the violent crime, as Gail thoroughly believed, then a savage monster could still be running around loose in the town, even after all this time had passed. That fact alone kept many in the local citizenry uneasy.

Gail took a deep breath, opened the library door and stepped aside to allow Detective Hudson and his cohorts to enter. Seated at one end of a long oak conference table, near a window at the far end of the room, was Damon Powell. The books and papers he was consulting were scattered about. He had removed his jacket, his tie was pulled loose, and one stubborn lock of dark hair drooped over his forehead.

The young man appeared to be lost in his work, and at first paid no attention to the group of people entering the room. Charlie Hudson stopped abruptly in front of him, blocking the thin late-afternoon light from the nearby window. Looking up in puzzlement, Damon took in the police detective, uniformed cops in tow, grinning down at him.

'What ... ?' Damon began, but didn't have a chance to finish his thought before Hudson interrupted him in a loud, author-itative voice.

'Damon Powell, you are under the arrest for the murder of Marilyn Leeann Watson. You have the right to remain silent. Anything you say will be taken down and may be used in a court of law. You may have an attorney present ... ' Hudson rattled through the Miranda warning as Damon sat stunned.

'Marilyn? What is this, some kind of a joke? She's perfectly fine. We had dinner last night and I took her back to her father's house. This must be a mistake.'

Gail moved forward as one of the policeman prodded Damon to his feet and pulled his hands back for cuffing. 'Damon,' she said, 'listen to me carefully. Do not say anything at all unless I'm present or Connie is. You're right, this has to be some kind of terrible mistake. We'll get to the bottom of it as soon as possible. In the meantime ... ' She reached out her hand to Hudson and glanced quickly at the warrant he grudgingly handed her. ' ... you'll need to go with them. You know the drill. Don't panic, and don't say anything — not one word — unless I'm there.'

Conrad Osterlitz, followed by Hugo, was

hurrying down the hall toward them as they exited the library, Damon being led out in handcuffs, and Hudson grinning broadly at all the consternation he'd caused.

'Gail! What on earth's going on? What is the meaning of this, Charlie?' Connie glowered at Hudson.

Gail waved the warrant at Connie, who grabbed it and perused it thoroughly before handing it to Hugo to read. She turned back to Hudson. 'Where's her father, Charlie? Have you talked to him? He could possibly give Damon an alibi.'

'Well that's just it, isn't it, Counselor?' Hudson gazed at them in satisfaction before dropping his bombshell. 'Harold Watson has gone missing, Ms. Brevard. Presumably he was abducted from his home shortly after his daughter was brutally murdered. We have to assume Mr. Powell may have had something to do with his disappearance, as well as the crime at hand. So no, your client, thus far, has no alibi.' He paused for effect before adding, 'And what's more, the M.O. for this killing is exactly the same as for the murder of Vivian Seymour. Your Mr. Powell was a busy boy last night, Counselor.

And I don't think he'll be able to worm his way out of this one quite as easily as he did before. People around here have very long memories.'

Gail stood back as Damon was led off. 'Well,' she said to Connie and Hugo, 'here's another fine mess.'

3

Hal Watson struggled to keep his composure and his wits about him.

The good thing was, he tried to remind himself, that he had survived the crash on the hillside and had managed to extricate himself from the car. That in itself was huge. He also had retrieved the gun — and he didn't think he had suffered any severe injuries during the accident. He was stiff and sore, but that was to be expected after such an ordeal.

On the minus side, he was still at the bottom of the ravine, night was coming on rapidly, and it was threatening to storm — and he had no idea where in the hell he was.

He also had no idea if his captor was dead or had merely been knocked unconscious, so even though he had the advantage of the gun, that threat was still uppermost in his mind. He must get away from the car as quickly as possible.

He glanced about, then peered at the darkening sky, trying to get his bearings. He could not even be sure which way was north. He only knew that when they had headed out of the city on Highway 89 and on into the wilderness, he had quickly lost all sense of direction with the frequent turnings on the narrow fire road.

He had never been much enamored of country life, having been raised in the city. He had never even belonged to the Boy Scouts as a lad. He had been completely wrapped up in his father's grand ambitions for his future. Had stuck to the books, acquired a decent education, and had gone to work ... all in the city. And the fact was, he had never camped out anywhere, either. Once his captor had directed him out of the city proper, he was at the total mercy of the crazy person brandishing a weapon in the back seat of his car.

He tried in vain not to think of the disastrous scene they'd left back at his house before he had been forced at gunpoint into the car. *Put it straight out of your mind*, he told himself. After all, what was done was done. There would be time for reflection and mourning later.

A part of him didn't really want to survive right now. It would be much easier to lie down right here, on this cold, cold ground, and allow the elements to take him away from his pain. But there was an even more compelling drive forcing him onward. If he didn't survive, who would be left to tell the story of what had actually happened? And the story must be told. Justice must prevail. It was in his DNA to see this vicious cycle through to the end.

Survive he must. And that required some action. Movement. It required that he not give up just yet. But he was stuck here, at the site of the car crash, with no clear idea of which way to go. Trying to pull himself together, he looked about carefully and gave it some thought.

Was there anything still in the car he might find useful? There might be some tools in the trunk, but he hesitated to take the time to look. Also, if his tormentor somehow regained consciousness in the meantime, he might have to muster the strength to fight off yet another attack … and he doubted he had the energy left

21

to do that.

No. It was far better to try and get out of this remote canyon and as far away from the automobile wreck as possible. Hopefully he could find shelter of some sort along the way. Were there any summer cabins around here? He had no idea. But the sooner he began his upward trek out of here, the better.

As the lone figure began struggling and scrabbling up the long climb to the embankment and the road above, the snow began floating down in earnest: soft, heavy, fluffy flakes, in a steady stream, quickly and quietly laying a thick disguising blanket over all. Soon, he realized, all evidence of the car crash and its aftermath would be obliterated from sight — including the single trace of footprints moving uncertainly up the hillside.

In time, there would be no record left of what had happened here.

4

As Damon was led back down the hall toward the firm's reception area, Gail hung behind and conferred anxiously with Connie. 'What do you think?' she said. 'Has Charlie lost it completely? What in the world has happened?' The words tumbled out of her mouth all at once, uncharacteristically jumbled.

Connie stood still a moment, gazing at the departing police brigade jostling their unwilling captive along. 'Obviously *something* has happened. We'll know more once they file their warrant and begin to interrogate Damon. One of us needs to be there with him, and I suggest it be you. You have a good rapport with him. Just keep him from saying too much until we can get the full story. Hugo's already got a head start on this. Let him do his job and track down as many hard facts as he can.'

'I think we need to find Hal as soon as possible. If something's happened to

Marilyn, he'll need all our support now.'

Hal Watson was a criminal defense attorney in private practice in Cathcart. Gail had known him for quite a few years, and she and Connie had called on him for consultation more than once. She respected his experience and acumen, and had no hesitation in coming to his assistance if she could. Marilyn, his only daughter, was studying law with an eye to joining her father's practice one day. She was also Damon Powell's fiancée.

'Let's let Hugo do his job,' Connie said again. 'He'll probably be able to find Hal quicker than anyone, including the police, and the sooner he gets his people on the job, the better. We both know that forty-eight hours is the maximum leeway before a missing person's trail can go cold.'

Gail was silent a moment, thinking hard. Then she said, 'Do you think we'd better call on Charles? I don't know about you, but my court calendar is full right now. Most of it is minor stuff, but there's the Del Monaco hearing coming up next week. I've done most of the prelim work and have the brief outlined on my computer.

24

I was reviewing it again this afternoon, as a matter of fact. But someone will need to be in court on Monday, or we'll face another delay. And Ralph Del Monaco won't be happy about that.' The powerful Del Monaco family was in the midst of a bitter legal battle over patriarch Nino Del Monaco's fat estate, and his grandson Ralph was one of their major clients.

'You're right. Hopefully Charles can clear his slate and come out for a few weeks to help, at least until we know what we're dealing with.' Charles Walton was their associate and partner who ran the firm's Arizona office.

'If not, we're going to have to spell each other and do double duty with this new situation.' Gail shook her head. 'Just in case, can you look after Damon on Monday, while I handle the Del Monaco hearing?'

'I think so. All I have pending right now is that custody case for Lisa Mathews. I should be able to get a continuance on that. I don't think she'd mind. The longer Daryl Mathews has to twiddle his thumbs, the better, as far as Lisa's concerned.'

'All right. I think I'd better call Mother

right away and let her know we might be tied up for a while, just in case there's some issue brewing with Erle. I'm going to suggest that she ask Lucy to come stay with her for a bit. They always have a good time together, and Lucy's great with Erle.'

Lucy Verner, her mother's younger cousin, was bright, good-natured, and seemingly in great health. She was a retired nurse and lived in her family's home in a small farming community about 50 miles north of Cathcart. Between the two of them, Erle would be the perfect angel. Or at least that was what Gail hoped.

'That's a great idea,' Connie said. 'If necessary, tell her I can make a quick trip up to Grand View and get her. I hope she's free. It'd be a good solution.'

'All right.' Gail ducked into her office to grab her purse and briefcase. 'I'd better get going. I don't trust Charlie one little bit. I'd better get over there or he'll have Damon on the ropes.'

'Right. And, Gail … '

'Yes?' She looked back at him, one tendril of hair flying astray.

'Don't worry. We'll get through this.'

She waved at him, blew him a kiss, and strode out the main door. Time to do battle.

But first, she had to call her mother. Once in the elevator, she fumbled her phone out of her tote bag, hit the automatic number for M&E, and thrust the phone to her ear. Hopefully this conversation would go well.

★　★　★

'What do you mean, you don't know where he is?' Gail tried to keep the panic out of her voice but failed miserably. She stepped out of the elevator and made her way to a bench in the cavernous building lobby before adding, 'What happened?'

'Now, Gail, let's not jump to any conclusions.' Alberta Norris took a deep breath before continuing. 'I'm sure he's just playing one of his silly games with me. I thought he was doing his magic act in the playroom. I just shut my eyes for a minute …'

Gail took a deep breath and counted to three before responding. 'Mother, you know you can't nap while you're there alone with him during the day! You should wait until — '

'Yes, Gail, I know. You don't need to get short with me. I said I only shut my eyes for a minute. I thought he was just fine.'

Gail paused. The last thing she wanted to do right now was argue with her mother over this, with everything else on her plate. Why oh why did Erle have to pull this stunt right now? And why hadn't her mother been paying closer attention to him?

'I'm sorry, Mother,' she said in a calmer tone. 'I didn't mean it to sound that way. I'm just concerned. He isn't safe out on his own, you know that. We're going to have to get you some help.'

There was a brief silence, and Gail thought she detected crying sounds on the other end of the line. 'Mother, please! I just don't have time for all this. As I said, we've got this complicated situation going on with Damon, and we're short-handed as it is.'

She was alarmed to hear genuine sobs. 'So you're too busy with that … that murderer … to care about what's happened to your own brother?'

'Mother, I said I was sorry.' She didn't

bother to respond to the depiction of Damon as a murderer.

'You don't understand, Gail. Don't you think I know it was my fault he got away? I'm not stupid. I know I'm getting old, and it's getting harder for me to cope with these issues. But I don't think he could've gotten far. And, after all, it's not any worse than a young child running off somewhere to fool his mother. He'll be all right, I'm sure of it. I just thought you ought to know before I started out to look for him.'

'You're right, Mother,' Gail said in a calming tone. 'I'm sure Erle will be just fine. But I think it'd be better for you to stay there, just in case he shows up again. And he might be hiding somewhere in the house or yard. He's done that before. You stay right where you are and keep an eye out for him. I'll let Connie and Hugo know; they'll get some people on it right away. Like you said, he can't have gotten very far. He's probably just playing a trick on you. We'll find him and get him settled, then we'll talk about what we can do to keep this from happening again.'

'But ... ' Alberta's voice wavered off.

'Well, all right. I'll stay right here and wait. Maybe he'll come back on his own this time.'

Gail texted both Connie and Hugo with the news of Erle's disappearance, then pondered the dilemma as she headed out to Main Street to catch a cab to police headquarters. Connie was right, of course; they were going to have to make a change of some kind. Erle Norris was a child trapped in a man's body. Until recently, Alberta Norris had been fully capable of caring for and protecting her son. But this was not the first time in the past six months he had escaped her watch. The situation was deteriorating rapidly, and they would have to take action before something really terrible happened. Gail's own worse fear was not only the physical danger to her mentally challenged brother, as innocent and naïve as he was. No, her very worst concern, knowing how quickly his peaceful demeanor could turn to rage, and having seen the results of that rage, was the possible harm he might inflict on others, without really meaning to hurt them. And that, quite simply, could not be allowed.

Suddenly she knew exactly what had to be done. Once Erle was safe and back home again, she and Connie would need to have a long, painful talk with Alberta. She was certain her mother would be unhappy about the discussion, but it had to happen, and it would involve some difficult changes for all of them.

But change was necessary, wasn't it? All of life was full of change. And survival depended on how well you accepted and adapted to it. *Onward and upward*, she thought. *We'll get through this change, too.*

★ ★ ★

What a marvelous change! Erle kicked his feet in the first few inches of fallen snow on the black macadam in high spirits. No nasty mother to tell him, 'No, Erle! You mustn't do that!' No stuck-up sister who forgot all about him for days at a time. This was much better, out here in the woods, by himself, with no stupid adults around to spoil his fun.

Erle tried to whistle a song, something he heard someone else doing recently. What was it? How did it go? He hated it when he forgot stuff. It made him feel like a little kid. And he *wasn't* a little kid, was he? He was a big man now. Someone had told him that not very long ago, someone else....

He gave up trying to remember the raggedy tune and that other person. Maybe he would see that person out here in the woods, and they could play the game again. The funny, dangerous game no one else had ever played with him. An unfamiliar eagerness overwhelmed him as he thought hard about the strange but wonderful feeling the funny game gave him.

But he couldn't tell anyone else about it. No one else at all. Because the other person had warned him what would happen if he told. People would get hurt. No, people would *die* if he told. So whatever happened, and whatever anyone said to him — or asked him, he must not tell about the game. That had been drummed into his brain, and he dare not forget it.

An odd little chill came over him all of a sudden, and he shivered as he scuffed along in the icy ruts of the narrow country road. He felt something damp creeping into his shoes. Perhaps he should have worn his galoshes after all, since it was so wet and slushy out here. He liked that word, *slushy*. It had a funny, delicious taste to it, like cotton candy, the kind that made his nose wrinkle up like a bunny rabbit.

He stopped. Mother always said he should wear his galoshes and his overcoat and his hat if it was raining or snowing. And he didn't have any of those things with him today. He hadn't been thinking at all about things like that when he crept out of the house while Mother was sleeping.

Crept out quiet as a little mousie, he did. He grinned at the thought. He, Erle, dressed up in little mousie clothes! Creeping silently out of the house. Not getting caught....

But what did Mother know about anything? She was getting old ... older than 'thuslah, as they said in Sunday school. She didn't know *nothing*! He was just fine in his regular clothes and shoes. Just fine!

Suddenly a movement just out of the corner of his eye caught his attention. It must be a bird or some other kind of animal, fluttering about in the overgrown bushes near the road. He forgot all about the damp in his shoes; forgot about the tune he had been trying to remember, too. Was that thing in trouble? Should he go try to free it? Or should he just leave it to struggle alone? He grappled with this huge dilemma, much like the bird, or thing, or whatever it was, continued to thrash about in the undergrowth.

Why was it always so hard to make up his mind? he wondered. Why was everything always so hard for him? The other people in his life didn't seem to have this kind of problem. Mother, Gail, Connie. They all seemed to know exactly what they were going to do and when to do it. Not like him — always wondering what he was going to do, and if it would be okay to do it.

By now, given the huge dimension of the issue at hand, he had forgotten all about the other person and the game. They no longer existed for him, and he stood uncertainly in the middle of the road, brow furrowed, as he tried to decide what he was going to do next.

The thing struggling to free itself had now gained all of his attention. He began to move furtively, ever so slowly, toward the flapping noise in the brush at the side of the road. Now the icy dampness in his shoes was beginning to make his feet burn, almost as if they were on fire, and he brushed the drifting snowflakes away from his hatless brow impatiently. If Mother was here, or Gail, they would know what to do. They would fix everything for him and make it all better.

Angrily, he stomped his foot, and winced at the sudden sharp searing pain which made tears spring to his eyes. Suddenly he wished he was safe, warm and dry back at home, sitting in front of the bright crackling fire and playing games with Gail while Mother fixed hot cocoa and his favorite cinnamon toast, to take away the hurt and chill.

He limped on, whimpering under his breath to himself. But just as he was drawing near enough to the thrashing sound to get a good look at whatever it was, a dark figure stepped out from the trees on the other side of the road and called out to him, 'Erle! Erle Norris! Wait up a minute. We need to talk to you.'

Startled, he tripped and nearly fell down.

Something about the figure seemed menacing. He looked on in apprehension as the first figure was joined by a second. Who were they? Why did they know his name?

In a panic now, Erle began running, slipping and sliding through the icy sludge, trying to get away from the threatening dark forms giving chase. Just as they caught up with him and reached out to grab him, he fell face first into the snow and mud. An unearthly scream left his lips, as he felt hands grabbing at his clothing, pulling him back up and spinning him around roughly.

'What have you been up to, eh, Erle boy? What kind of nasty mischief have you been getting into, young man?'

'Wha …? What do you mean?' The words tumbled out. 'I don't know what you mean.' He began to whine, then burst into great, wet, heaving sobs.

Maybe change wasn't such a good thing after all, he thought as the two men led him to their car just over the rise and shoved him into the back seat.

5

Damon Powell wiped the sweat off his brow, then straightened and gazed into the camera for his mug shot. He tried to look calm and non-threatening, but the flash erupted before he was ready, and he had the distinct impression his photo would look just how he felt — hot, flustered and desperate.

'No, over here,' instructed the booking officer, handing him a packet of prison clothing and motioning him toward the holding area.

'All right — ' he began, determined to appear cooperative and reasonable.

'Shut up, punk.'

He quickly changed and handed his street clothes and personal belongings over and watched as they were catalogued and signed in. Then a guard led him down a narrow hall, shoved him into a small cubicle, and slammed the steel door shut. There was a cut-out in the upper panel of the door, but it was operable only from the outside.

Damon glanced around to take stock of his surroundings. A flimsy steel cot with one thin coverlet took up most of one wall. A small stainless-steel sink with one spigot was on the back wall, and a urinal was set into the far corner. One straight-backed chair faced a small metal table bolted to the opposite wall. There was scarcely room to turn around, and Damon immediately began to feel claustrophobic.

He stretched his arms and rubbed his hands together, trying to regain feeling in them. He sat down gingerly on the edge of the cot and tried to relax, but the strain of the last few hours wouldn't allow it.

The horror of it all had not sunk in yet. He was still trying to make sense of what the police detective had said about Marilyn. Dead? Impossible! He had spent a happy and relaxing early evening with her, dining at their favorite Italian restaurant — joking, laughing, with a few serious moments as they discussed the wonderful future they had planned together. They had eaten early, and he had taken her straight back to her father's house a little before dusk. They both had busy schedules, and had agreed to call it an evening so they could get a good night's sleep. He had kissed her on the porch — a sweet, long-lasting kiss — then waited while she unlocked the door.

Wait. That was the puzzle piece that didn't fit. The front door wasn't locked. They both had remarked on it.

'Dad must be getting forgetful,' she had said, turning the knob. She smiled. 'Too much on his mind, I expect. He usually isn't this lax.'

'Do you want me to come in and check things out, just to be sure?'

He remembered, now, the faint chill of apprehension that had come over him.

'No. I'm sure everything's fine. He's probably still working in his office. He might have stepped out on the porch to catch a breath of air, then forgot to latch the door when he went back in.'

'All right, if you're sure,' he said.

He had hesitated a moment, then lightly brushed the top of her head with his hand and swung off the top step as she stepped inside and shut the door firmly behind her.

39

The lock clicked. That he was sure of.

He had to tell Gail as soon as possible. He glanced anxiously down the brightly lit hall leading back to the booking room. Where was she? She should have been here by now.

He was suddenly scared to death, and deeply saddened, at the thought of what was to come. He had been through all this before. It had changed his life completely. Now, he knew, his life was going to change completely again ... and he had no control over what was about to happen to him.

* * *

Damon, seated on the cot in a deep reverie, was startled a while later when the steel door suddenly clanked open.

'C'mon. Yer mouthpiece is here.'

Damon stood still while the cuffs and shackles were put in place, then followed the taciturn guard awkwardly out into the corridor as directed. He knew enough not to argue or hesitate. *Pick your battles* was the phrase that echoed in his mind, and he obeyed.

Gail looked up when the orange-suited prisoner shuffled in and took a seat across from her at a pitted metal table. The cubicle was small, square, and painted a sickly institutional green. A faint odor of fear, sweat and Lysol permeated the room.

The guard removed Damon's handcuffs and gave Gail a brief nod. 'I'll be right outside, ma'am, in case you need anything.' He glared meaningfully at Damon.

'Thank you, officer, I'll be just fine,' she said. She waited a beat, until the guard left, clanking the door shut behind him. Then: 'You okay?'

'As okay as I can be, under the circumstances. Gail, I forgot to mention it, but would … could you let my parents know what's happened? I try to go out there a couple of times a week. If they don't hear from me, they'll start to worry. Tell them not to try to come here just yet. I'll get together with them just as soon as I possibly can. Please.'

Gail was alarmed at how swiftly his demeanor had changed, from the relaxed and competent young man she'd chatted with yesterday to this new Damon, pinch-faced and desperate. 'Of course I will. I'll take care of that just as soon as we're through here and have a little more information,' she said, then added, 'They haven't tried to interrogate you yet, have they?'

'No. They brought me in, fingerprinted me, photographed me, then stuck me in the holding cell. No one's tried to talk to me since I've been here.'

'Good. Now listen to me, and listen hard. Don't offer them a thing. Not one thing. Do you hear? Hugo's begun his own investigation. We're pulling the whole team together on this one, Damon. We're not going to let you go down.'

'Gail — I thought of something I have to tell you. Let Hugo know.' He lowered his voice and spoke in a quiet monotone, hoping any bugs in the room wouldn't be able to pick it up. 'I think whoever did this was already in the house when I left. Marilyn tried to use her key, but the door was unlocked, which was totally unlike Hal. He had no idea when we were coming back, so there wouldn't have been any reason for him to unlock the door before she came home.'

Gail nodded. 'All right. That's a good piece of evidence. I'll get Hugo going on that possibility right away. Of course the cops will have been all over the scene, looking for fingerprints and anything else. But as soon as we get the all-clear, Hugo will go in and look for anything they might've missed. I suspect they've already fingered you for this, so they won't be looking very hard for evidence to prove otherwise. That gives us a bit of an advantage.'

'I could kick myself for not going in with her,' he said, 'just to check things out. She thought Hal might have stepped out on the porch for a breath of air or something, then just forgot to lock the door when he went back in. I don't buy that, though, and didn't at the time. I should've insisted — '

'You can't beat yourself up over this, Damon. It won't change things, and it won't do us any good down the road. Keep your wits about you, and keep trying to think of anything, anything at all, that might shed some light on this.'

'I'm trying, Gail. I'm honestly trying.

But I keep dredging up the memories of the Seymour trial, and it scares the hell out of me. I feel like someone is out to get me, for whatever reason. And I don't understand why.'

Just then there was a brief rap, followed by the scrape of the door opening. 'They're ready to interrogate you,' the guard announced, motioning to Damon to stand and place his hands behind his back once again. 'You coming?' he added to Gail.

'Yes, definitely,' she said.

As the guard led Damon out and down the hall in the other direction, away from the cells, Gail was directed a different way, towards the public section of the night court. She tried to gather her thoughts as she prepared for the brief preliminary hearing to decide on bail.

So someone had been in the house when Damon and Marilyn had gotten there last evening. Probably had already subdued Hal, and waylaid his daughter as soon as she entered the house. She might've been killed instantly, or tortured over the evening.

Her stomach revolted at the thought. Poor Hal. What a tragic situation. But where was he? Was Marilyn's father dead, too? Or had he survived to tell the tale?

★　★　★

'Oof!' Damon had more or less anticipated the quick, hard jab to his solar plexus, but he was not fast enough to maneuver away in time to avoid the main thrust. He tripped awkwardly over his own ankle shackles and stumbled into the rough stucco wall of the back walkway leading from the holding cells to the interrogation rooms of the county jail.

He paused and bent over for a moment to catch his breath, and tried to ignore the dull throb starting somewhere in the middle of his belly. He would have a helluva bruise there tomorrow. No doubt about it.

'Watch it there,' rumbled the guard, grabbing at Damon's manacled hands and pulling him back to an upright position. 'Gotta be careful in here, *Mr.* Powell. Lotsa *rules and regulations* here, if ya get my drift. Fella could get hurt real bad, if he don't watch his Ps and Qs.'

'Yes sir,' Damon said, gazing steadily at

a point about two inches below the man's stubbled chin. He was well aware of the animosity against him, and fully expected a little man-handling before things settled down. 'Yes sir,' he repeated. 'I just tripped. I'll try not to do that again.'

'You better believe you'll try.' Jim Richards had been around a long time and knew just how much leeway he had in dealing with this riff-raff. 'I ain't got no time to babysit yer sorry ass,' he added with a sniff of disdain. ''Sides, we ain't got no sympathy for you and yer kind. Lady-killer!' The latter was hissed directly into Damon's ear.

Damon continued to look down, stoically ignoring the other man's jibes. He was at a definite disadvantage here, but was determined to survive this debacle. He hoped Gail would be able to convince them to allow bail. Otherwise ...

This was not the same Damon Powell who had been hauled before the bar five years earlier. In the intervening time he had pulled himself together, made amends with his parents, gone back to school, and gained the trust, and even friendship, from people he admired and respected. And Marilyn

— his dear Marilyn — had become the love of his life. She was his reason for being. She had been the one he wanted at his side through all that life had to offer. And now, according to all reports, she had been viciously and senselessly murdered.

Why? Why me? Why now?

Those questions and many more were bubbling up in his mind as he numbly followed Richards down the not-so-clean, musty-smelling corridor where he would meet up with Gail and his accusers. And endure more questions he couldn't answer, and more insinuations and innuendo about his past. He shook his head dumbly like a gored ox being led to its final appointment. Looked like no matter how he tried, he just couldn't catch a break in this world.

The duo made their clanking way through several intervening security doors before Richards finally came to a halt. 'Hold up, now. Don't move a muscle, hear? Or you'll be sorry you ever got up this morning.' Pointing Damon face forward towards the sickly green wall, the guard knocked then opened the door into the largest interrogation room. He pulled his prisoner roughly about and shoved him forward.

'Here's Prisoner Powell, Sir,' Richards announced, sketching a quick salute and addressing the senior detective seated at the table.

'Thank you, Jim,' said Charlie Hudson, motioning to the vacant seat on the far side of the table. 'Take a seat, Mr. Powell,' he added. Then, for benefit of the recorder, he said, 'Damon Powell has just entered the room for interrogation. Also present are Detective Charles Hudson, Sergeant Arthur Rolfe, and prisoner's counsel, Ms. Gail Brevard.'

There was a brief scuffling of chairs as everyone got settled, and the prisoner's handcuffs were removed. Gail looked anxiously at Damon's strained face before staring pointedly at Jim Richards. Damon vaguely shook his head at her, trying to avoid any unpleasantness.

'Are you all right?' she asked.

'I'm fine, Gail. Just let it go.' He was clutching his midsection, obviously in pain.

Hudson ignored this brief exchange and shuffled a few papers in front of him before glancing up at Jim Richards hovering near the door. 'That'll be all, Jim. We'll call you when we need you again.'

'Yes sir. I'll be right outside the door if you need me.' He glared at Damon, now seated at the table next to Gail, then ducked outside.

Once the door was closed, Hudson looked up at Damon. 'State your name for the record.'

'Damon Powell.'

'And you reside within the township of Cathcart?'

'Yes.'

'And what is your occupation?'

'I'm employed part-time by the Goldthwaite agency. I'm also attending law school and interning for Osterwitz and Brevard while I study for the bar exam.' This last was uttered with an air of pride. He looked the detective squarely in the eye.

Hudson nodded, paused, and checked his records again. 'What were you doing on the evening of November the third, between the hours of five p.m. and midnight?'

Powell glanced at Gail, who nodded. No point in stonewalling here. All of this was pretty straightforward.

'I was having a very early dinner at the Napoli Restaurant in Midtown with my fiancée, Marilyn Watson. We finished our meal at approximately five p.m., and then I drove her to her father's house in Long Hills. We arrived there by five thirty or a little after, and I dropped her off. Then I returned to my apartment back in Midtown. I studied for a while, watched the news, then went to bed.'

'What did you and Miss Watson discuss during your dinner?'

The small recorder spun away to Charlie Hudson's right, and he referred from time to time to a thick folder in front of him.

Damon glanced at Gail, seated next to him. She nodded. This was safe enough.

'We just chatted. We both had to be up early this morning, so we didn't spend a lot of time there. We ate a light meal, and talked about what was going on at work and our classes. Things like that. Nothing of any importance.'

'Were you aware that her father would be waiting up for her at home?'

'We weren't that late. As I said, I think

50

we got to the house by five or a little after. I saw her to the door, then left. I didn't see Hal, but I assumed he was inside the house, either working in his office or having his own dinner and watching TV.'

'Did you have any cross words with Miss Watson or any kind of argument during dinner?'

Gail held up her hand and stopped him. 'Mr. Powell has already characterized their discussion as benign. I don't think he needs to describe the conversation further than that.'

Hudson grimaced and glanced down at the folder in front of him. 'Do you carry a firearm, Mr. Powell?'

'Don't answer that, Damon.'

'Ms. Brevard,' Charlie said, turning to Gail in exasperation, 'that's a simple enough question, and one that Mr. Powell should be happy to answer.'

Before Gail could say anything further, Damon interrupted. 'No, I do not carry a weapon of any kind. I certainly wouldn't have been carrying one yesterday.'

Gail cringed. She had not wanted the questioning to veer off into this territory, but at least Damon had had the sense to answer in the negative.

'Where and when did you and Miss Watson meet yesterday, and what time exactly did you arrive at the Napoli Restaurant?'

'Well, let's see. I made reservations for four thirty. My last class was out at three thirty, but the traffic between Midtown and Long Hills is murder about then.' Damon shook his head and cringed at his unintentional use of the word *murder*. After a moment, he continued. 'It took me about half an hour to get to the Watson house. Mari — Miss Watson had been working with her father in his law office yesterday afternoon. The two of them drove home together, but I'm not sure of the time. I believe she'd changed clothes before I picked her up at approximately four o'clock or so. She met me in front of the house, and Mr. Watson didn't come out, so I didn't see him at all. I just assumed he was still inside. I actually suggested he join us, but he said he had some things he wanted to work on through the evening, so he took a rain check.'

'So you're telling me you never saw Hal

Watson at all yesterday? What about during the day?'

'No. Yesterday was a full day for me at school. I had two classes, and I took advantage of the time between them to study in the library and work on some papers that were due. If I'd been working at the law firm that day or running errands for Hugo, I might've run into him, maybe at the court house. But that wasn't the case yesterday. As I said, he didn't come out of the house when I picked up his daughter, and he didn't make an appearance when I brought her home either. So no, I didn't see him at all yesterday.'

Gail had been jotting down notes while Damon spoke. He had told her all this earlier, but she wanted to keep a clear picture in her mind of the sequence of events. Everything would depend on Damon's story coming across clearly.

'Now let's move on to the events following your arrival at the Watson house after the dinner date. What did you and Miss Watson do and say between the time you arrived together and the time you say you left alone?'

Gail held up a hand again. 'I believe Mr. Powell has already explained exactly what occurred when he left Miss Watson at her father's house.' She looked at Damon and shook her head. 'Don't answer this one, Damon. He's fishing.'

'Ms. Brevard, you don't want to get into a situation where you could be accused of hampering an investigation.' Hudson glared at her.

'I'm sorry, Detective. But if you'll play back that tape, I'm sure you'll realize you've already asked a version of that question, and Mr. Powell has answered it fully. Now if you have nothing else at this time, I'd like to seek bond for my client.'

'One more question, if you please.' Hudson glanced down again at his notes. 'Where did you go after you say you left the Watson house last evening?'

This time Gail remained silent. She already knew the answer, and it would not harm Damon.

'As I said, I went straight back to my apartment in Midtown. I was scheduled to work for Hugo today, and I wanted to get some more done on those school papers

I mentioned. I worked a bit, watched the news on TV, took a shower and went to bed. I slept soundly until about six this morning, when I got up and got ready for the day. I fixed myself some breakfast, ate and cleared up the dishes, then left the apartment about eight a.m. Once again the traffic was heavy, and it took me about twenty or thirty minutes to get to the office. Hugo had called a staff meeting for eight thirty, and I got there just in time to attend. He can confirm that fact.'

Damon stopped and sat back, drained. The stress of the interview was etched into his face, and his usual happy-go-lucky manner had disappeared completely.

'Did you see or speak to her father at the house before leaving?'

Gail started to object, but thought better of it. Damon had already answered this question, but let Charlie spin his wheels if he wanted.

'No, as I told you before. We both had early classes the next morning. I walked her up to the door, said goodnight and left.'

'Did you see her enter the house?'

Damon paused and thought back. 'Yes,

I saw her enter the house. She stopped in the doorway and waved me on, then turned, made her way into the house, and closed the door behind her.' He swallowed and put his head down in agony. If only he *had* stayed long enough to see her safely inside. If he had just gone in and spoken to Hal. If he had just made sure, absolutely sure, everything was all right. He would never be able to forgive himself for his lapse in judgment. He completely disregarded the fact that the same horrible fate might have befallen him if he had entered that house of horror that night. As far as he was concerned, he might as well be dead right now anyway.

Gail spoke up. 'I don't think my client has anything further to add about this, Detective. There should be a record at the Napoli of his dinner out with the victim before returning her to her father's home and care. I assume you're making every effort to find Mr. Watson,' she added. 'He can provide proof of Mr. Powell's statement. Without any concrete evidence to the contrary, it must be assumed that events transpired just as my client states. He had an uneventful dinner out with his fiancée, returned her home, watched her enter the house without problem, then went back to his own apartment, where he spent the rest of the evening studying.'

Charles Hudson stared her down. 'But that's just the problem, Counselor. Hal Watson disappeared from his home that very evening. Presumably he witnessed the fatal attack on his daughter and, as a result, was taken to some other place where he is either being held prisoner or has become a second victim in this heinous crime. Until, and if, Watson is found, Damon Powell remains a person of interest to us, and we are going to act accordingly.'

Gail abruptly changed the subject. 'Who's on tonight, Charlie?' she said, glancing at her watch. 'I intend to request bail, and the sooner we get out of here, the sooner you can get back to looking for Hal.'

'You might have a little trouble with that, Counselor,' Hudson sneered. 'Ballou's on, I think. Lots of luck there.' Aaron Ballou was a law-and-order judge, well-known for his tough stance on crime.

'Well, let's see,' Gail said. 'The first thing

I'll request is a complete physical exam for my client. He appears to be in some discomfort from the handling he's had in just a few hours under your care here.'

Damon grimaced and Hudson sighed. He made a pretense of shuffling through his papers again. 'Now, Counselor, no need to get on your high horse. I suspect your client tripped and fell. Right, Powell?'

Damon nodded, but Gail ignored the exchange. 'Are we done here, Detective? The sooner we get into night court, the better.'

Charles Hudson thought a moment. He knew old Jim Richards well enough to acknowledge the guard had probably handled Powell a little too roughly. If he admitted it, he'd done the same thing with this very prisoner five years ago — the first time he'd encountered him. Too bad he hadn't saved the taxpayers a little dough and finished the job then, he mused. Public sentiment at the time was certain Powell had offed the lovely and popular young Vivian Seymour. There would have been a brief enquiry, followed by a complete vindication of his actions. Wag, his partner at the time, would've stood behind him 100 percent, he was sure of that. Yes, it was too bad something couldn't be done now to push the balance to his favor. He would have to think about that a bit more.

Gail stood up. 'That's enough, Detective. We're through now. Will you please release my client for the bond hearing? I'll be requesting that he be released on his own recognizance. He has ties to the community and is no risk for flight. My firm will vouch for that.'

Charlie Hudson knew when to back down. There would be plenty more opportunities to question Damon Powell. He would see to that. 'All right,' he said, motioning to Jim Richards, lurking just outside the glass-windowed door. 'Let's get this show on the road.'

Hudson conferred with Richards briefly, then motioned attorney and client forward. 'Judge Ballou is available in fourteen. We'll see if he agrees with your request or not.'

Thank heavens, Gail thought. She wasn't at all sure she could convince that old curmudgeon Ballou that Damon Powell was not a risk for flight, but she would sure give it her all. She gave Damon a reassuring smile as Richards cuffed him again for the parade down to night court. With any luck, she could get him released on O.R. She was furious at his appearance when Richards had dragged him into the interrogation room. Damon wasn't talking, but she was sure he had been handled roughly, and a physical exam would prove it. That might work in her favor, as she tried to convince Ballou her client was not safe in the general population.

She could also mention the fact that too much publicity about her client being held in connection with the unsolved murder would give her plenty of ammunition to request a change of venue, a ploy all judges loathed to review. Yes, that just might work. Then they all could get back to looking for Hal Watson, wherever he might be.

6

True to Gail's instincts, Judge Ballou had listened to her plea for a physical exam for her client, looked sharply at Damon's pinched pale face, and glared at Charlie Hudson.

Clarissa Holmes, the young ADA, offered little or no rebuttal to Gail's argument. This was routine, so far as she was concerned. She yawned. There was a short line of prisoners waiting in the holding area. She might even get off early tonight.

'Is this true, Detective?' Ballou said. 'Has your prisoner been injured?'

Hudson shrugged. 'I have no idea, your honor,' he said. 'Prisoners often stumble or fall when being transferred from the holding facility to interrogation. If so, he said nothing to me about it.'

Ballou gazed down at the docket in front of him. 'Has the prisoner agreed to a DNA swab?'

'Yes, your honor. And he's been

fingerprinted as part of the booking procedure.'

'Ms. Brevard,' the judge said, turning to Gail, 'what assurances can you give me that your client is not a risk for flight?'

'Mr. Powell has strong ties in the community, your honor. He is a lifetime resident, and his parents and other family members are residents here as well. He is a law student in good standing, is gainfully employed by the Goldthwaite Agency, and is an intern in good standing with my firm. I will provide my personal assurance and bond that Mr. Powell will comply with the court's orders, and I will also stake the reputation of my firm that he will not be a risk for flight.' Gail paused. 'Your honor, I have known Mr. Powell for the past five years. He has worked diligently to acquire an education and improve himself. In all my experience with him, I have never had a moment's doubt concerning his character, and I have the utmost confidence in his integrity and reliability.'

Damon lowered his head and blinked back tears of relief and gratitude. To hear Gail utter such words of support at this time moved him more than he could express.

Ballou pondered her words. 'Very well, Counselor. We'll give it a try. But mark my words, you'd better be correct about this. I will hold you to your statement. Mr. Powell,' he added, 'see that you honor your attorney's trust in you.'

'Yes, your honor.' Damon Powell straightened up as best he could and spoke firmly. 'I certainly will. And thank you, your honor. I am very grateful.'

'Very well,' Ballou said. 'Move along now. I have other cases to hear.'

★ ★ ★

Gail was relieved to see Hugo Goldthwaite just outside the booking area, where she had gone to wait for Damon's release. 'He's being released on bond,' she said. 'He got bounced around a bit in there, but in the end it worked in our favor. I don't think Ballou wanted to risk any kind of publicity about police brutality. What's the matter?' She had just realized that the detective was shaking his head and looking at her with a pained expression which belied his normally unflappable demeanor.

'Oh, hell, Gail,' he began.

'What's wrong? Have they found Hal Watson? What is it?'

'No, no, nothing like that. It's Erle.'

'Erle? What ... what's happened?' Gail grabbed Hugo's arm in consternation. 'Is he all right?'

'He's fine. Well ... yes, he's fine. But a couple of off-duty officers picked him up and took him to the hospital to be checked out for frostbite.'

'But he's all right?'

'Yes; but when I talked to the officers, they told me they found ...'

'Go on, Hugo. You're scaring me. What in the world are you talking about?'

'When they stripped him down to make sure he was all right, they found ... they found some marks on his back ...'

'Marks? What kind of marks?'

'Well, they appeared to be scratches ... welts, really, from very recent scratches. Gail, they looked like fingernail scratches.'

Gail stared at Hugo. The implication sank in. 'Fingernail scratches? But ... but how could that be? Who would have ... '

She thought a moment. Could they be the result of an altercation with her mother? She couldn't believe the idea, and put it immediately out of her head. But who else would have had such intimate contact with her brother? He wasn't around that many people. Mostly neighbors and family friends. People she'd known most of her life. People who would never harm someone like Erle.

But what if he had met someone new, someone unknown to the rest of his circle, while out on one of these sprees of his? How many times had this happened now? She had to think back and count in her mind the number of times Alberta had called with the news that Erle had, once again, 'run away.' And had her mother admitted it each and every time? What if she had failed to mention all the separate instances Erle had managed to give her the slip — for a few minutes, for an hour … for half a day, perhaps?

'Is he still at the hospital?'

'Yes. But he's going to be released into our care in a little while. Connie's with him right now.' He paused before adding, 'The

65

problem is, with this other situation … '
Hugo glanced over at the swinging double
doors to the booking area. '… the officers
are saying now they need to report this to
the authorities; take a closer look at Erle
and his activities.'

'What?' Gail couldn't believe her ears.
'Why would they want to do that? He's a
child.' Then the full implication of what
Hugo had just said hit her. Her man-child
brother was over six feet tall, hefty, and
emotionally unstable. If he had scratches on
his back inflicted by somebody, the impli-
cations were many and disturbing. 'Surely
they're not going to arrest him.'

'I don't have any idea, Gail. All I know
is, we may have more than one mystery on
our hands. We're going to need all the help
we can get.'

'Good thing Charles is coming in tomorrow evening. Hugo, I hate to ask you this
given everything else, but do you think you
could pick him up at the airport?'

'Of course. But let's get Damon back
to his apartment as soon as he's released.
Do you think he'll be all right there for the
night?'

'Oh, I don't know, Hugo. Well, I guess he'll have to be. He said he doesn't want to go to his parents' house. He knows they're going to be upset about all this, asking all kinds of questions. I think he just wants some time alone to come to grips with this thing. I'll try to meet with him tomorrow. We need to go over every detail of last night. Something's not right here.' She shook her head, adding, 'All right. Let's drop Damon off then get back to the hospital. Connie and I can go on to Mother's and get her prepared for this new bombshell. Do you mind waiting for Erle to be released?'

'Sounds like a plan. Oh, here comes Damon now. Let's go. Got a lot of turf to cover tonight.'

'That we do.' She looked anxiously at Damon as he joined them. 'Are you all right?'

'Yes, I am now.' He was moving stiffly, and his face was pale and drawn with fatigue, but he headed towards the door unassisted. 'Come on. Let's get out of this hell hole.'

★ ★ ★

'Mother,' Gail called out as she entered the Norris family home near Long Hills an hour or so later, 'where are you? We need to talk.'

'Out here, in the sunroom,' answered Alberta Norris. She looked up in anticipation as her daughter and Conrad Osterlitz came into the comfortable little sitting area off the formal living room. She spent most of her time in here these days. The front of the house was shaded during much of the day, but this cozy spot captured as much light and warmth as the late-afternoon sun offered this time of year.

Gail moved forward and kissed her mother's brow. Alberta Norris was still a handsome woman, with an aristocratic air that belied her normal good humor. Today, however, her brow was furrowed, and Gail suspected she had been crying.

'Good news,' Gail began. 'Erle is safe.'

'Oh, thank God,' Alberta said. She visibly relaxed her shoulders, and tears appeared in the troubled blue-green eyes. 'Where is he? Did you bring him home?' She peered anxiously behind Connie, standing in the doorway, hoping to catch a glance of her wayward son.

'No. But let me explain. I don't want you to jump to conclusions or fret over this.' Gail pulled up a chair and sat beside her mother, as Connie stepped forward into the room and took a seat opposite on the sofa. 'He was picked up by a couple of off-duty police officers way out by Rook's Creek,' she continued, ignoring her mother's gasp of disbelief. 'Yes, I know. He's never gone that far before, at least as far as we know.'

'But where is he? They didn't put him in jail, did they? What had he done, that they arrested him for?' Alberta pounded on her chair arm in frustration. 'Why didn't I watch him better? Why wasn't I more careful?'

'He hasn't been arrested, Mother, and the only reason they picked him up was because they recognized him and were concerned he might get hurt. You know, it had started to snow, and he only had street clothes on. They were worried about frostbite, so they took him to Community to get checked out. That's all.'

'But why didn't you stay with him, Gail?

You know how he is with strangers.'

'It's all right, Alberta,' Connie spoke up. 'We've talked to him, and he agreed to let Hugo stay with him while they made sure he was all right. We thought you'd want to know, so we came on ahead to tell you about it. Hugo will bring him over as soon as they release him. It shouldn't be long.'

Alberta sat silently, staring out the window at the snowy expanse that was her side yard. In the summer there would be roses, and birds flying about, and butterflies. Erle loved looking out at that scene, keeping an eye out for the occasional bunny or squirrel. But today there were only snowdrifts piling up under a gloomy sky. Only occasionally did an errant sunbeam break through, and even those were scarce, now that the afternoon was fading into dusk. *Sort of like my life now*, Alberta thought. *Gloomy, with little sunlight offered at the end of my day.*

She looked back at Gail and Connie. They were good people. She couldn't manage without them. That she knew. And she was very grateful for their concern and care. But they were still too young to understand how difficult it was to relinquish control over one's own existence — nor would they understand, she reasoned, until they came to that point in life themselves.

'So what's the plan?' she said, bracing herself. She knew, without a doubt, that this was going to be a difficult conversation.

Just then there was a swift knock at the front door, and Hugo poked his head in. 'Hi. It's just me and Erle,' he called out. 'You guys out in the sunroom?'

Connie went to greet them and led the way back.

'Oh my, Erle,' Alberta said, taking in her son's sodden clothing, his damp hair and reddened nose and ears. 'Let's go in to the fire and get you a blanket and some hot cocoa.'

'Yes, Mommy,' Erle said, moving into her embrace.

They stood there a moment, like a frozen pietà, before Alberta Norris shooed them all back into the living room where a warm fire blazed away. Settling Erle in a comfortable overstuffed chair before the flames, she bustled about, wrapping him in a crocheted afghan, before hurrying out to the kitchen to prepare the promised hot chocolate.

Hugo spoke quietly to Connie and Gail for a moment or two, then took his leave. He had operatives out trying to track down any information on the missing Hal Watson. It would be a busy night for the detective. 'I'm going back to the office for a few hours,' he said to his partners as he headed for the door. 'I've got a bunch of people working on this thing 24/7 now, and we'll keep at it until we find Hal.'

'I don't know what we'd do without you,' Gail said. 'If we can't find Hal, Damon's defense is going to be difficult. There's so much sentiment against him, I can't see how he can get a fair trial here.'

'We should file for a change of venue as soon as possible,' Connie agreed. 'If we can't find Hal quickly — and alive, this case could be one of the biggest challenges we've ever faced.'

7

A lone figure struggled, one precarious step at a time, up the slippery slope heading from the cavernous ravine below to the snow-filled fire trail above. More often than not, it seemed to him, it took two steps backwards to regain one firm step forward.

The flakes were coming down rapidly now: large, soft and wet. They soon covered the lightly clad climber's hair, and he was forced repeatedly to brush the wet blobs back from his eyes in order to see. Glancing back, he could barely make out the wreck of the car. Soon it would be covered completely, and invisible from the road above. The faint tracks of his footsteps in the snow would also be obliterated, he realized, leaving no hint that anyone had been here recently.

He stopped to rest at one point, and nearly fell to the ground when a sudden muscle spasm gripped his chest. A heart attack? *No!* he shouted to himself. He wouldn't succumb to it. He had to get up to the road and find shelter. He had to stay alive in order to inform the authorities what had happened.

And what *had* happened? An intense rush of grief overwhelmed him. What was the point? What did any of it matter now? Would it make any difference at all, in the grand scheme of things, for him to somehow remain alive in order to testify as to the truth of what had happened? But the realist in him prevailed. Yes, it mattered.

Resolutely, he began plodding upward again. It was cold, so cold. He had come away with his feet shod in the old comfortable loafers and wearing nothing but a jogging suit. No hat or topcoat. Unthinkable garb for this time of year, with storms threatening like this. But he had had no choice, of course. Once that devil had overtaken him in the foyer, after he had stepped out on the porch for a brief moment to check the weather, everything that followed had been quick and to the point.

He rubbed the back of his head where he had been struck. Not hard enough to knock him out, but enough to convince him he had to comply with the instructions he was given. Now he wished he had fought back harder. It wouldn't have mattered if he died in the effort, if his actions might have changed the final outcome.

Fighting back the sobs, tears trailing down his face and leaving tracks in the bits of snowflake clinging there, he struggled onward and upward in desperation and with purpose. If he didn't make it up to the road, he knew he would surely die here on this cursed slope. And that he was not prepared to do just yet. He must survive in order to tell his story. He must make sure that justice would be done.

Hal Watson, after many fits and starts, finally pulled himself up and over the berm at the top of the cliff separating the narrow fire road from the chasm below. He rubbed his upper left arm. There was a dull ache spreading across his collarbone area, and he tried to shake it off. Must have pulled a muscle extricating himself from the car, he thought, trying to convince himself. He peered through the blinding snow, still falling steadily from the darkened sky. He could see nothing as he looked first one way, then the other along the narrow, half-overgrown road.

He tried to think rationally. He knew they had come up here from the left and had passed no sign of habitation at all. What was it his captor said? Something about 'It's not far now'? The devil must have had some nearby destination in mind, so he suspected there was some sort of building or shelter further along this road — although he could not be sure if it was on the road itself, or down a drive or smaller pathway leading off the road. If the latter, he would certainly be out of luck, since visibility was almost zero now. He could barely make out the edges of the roadway, and the only thing that actually delineated it was the lack of trees in its path.

Resolutely, he struck out to the right and trudged along through the deepening drifts. He was freezing, and his smooth-soled shoes slipped in the icy slush. Still, he tried to set a regular pace, forced all thought from his mind save moving forward, and glanced frequently around for some sign of habitation.

8

Late the next afternoon, Charles Walton paced nervously back and forth in front of the Hathaway Airport terminal, a battered briefcase in one hand, and tugging his carry-on with the other. He felt nervous and bedraggled, sweating profusely under his topcoat in spite of the glowering skies and scattered snowflakes drifting down to melt harmlessly on the asphalt.

A familiar sedan pulled into the next available slot in front of him, and he rushed toward the opening trunk to deposit his bags.

'Good flight?' Hugo reached out a hand to help steer the luggage in. He slammed the trunk shut with a solid 'whump,' and trotted back to the driver's side.

Charles climbed in beside him, heaving a sigh of relief. He and Hugo were buddies, and he always felt better in the detective's company. 'It was all right. A couple of unhappy babies, and pretty crowded. But, yeah, can't complain.'

There was a moment of companionable silence between the two friends, as Hugo maneuvered out of the parking space and back into the line of traffic circling the airport.

'What the hell's going on, Hugo?' Charles glanced at the man beside him, checking traffic and pulling onto the parkway. 'I couldn't believe my ears when Connie called me about this. I thought all this had been settled long ago. They can't reopen the old case. That would be double jeopardy.'

'They're saying this is the same M.O. as the old case, which makes Damon 'a person of interest.' They didn't mention any connection to the Seymour case in the charges, probably because Damon was intimately involved with Marilyn. They don't have to make a connection, if they can tie him to this case without it.'

'But they were engaged to be married. From all accounts, theirs was a very happy relationship. He seemed to have turned his life completely around over the past few years. I know the few times I've talked to Hal, he seemed very happy for them. No reservations whatsoever.'

'Yeah. I think they're going to have to prove motive. By the way, are you staying with Floyd and Nancy?'

'Yes. I did call them, to let them know I was coming to town, and Floyd insisted on it. I thought maybe it'd be better if I stayed at the hotel, but he wouldn't hear of it. I know this whole thing is going to be rough on them, and I don't know, it might even be a conflict of interest for me to stay with them. I guess I can move at some point, if it feels necessary.'

Floyd and Nancy Seymour were Charles's aunt and uncle, as well as being major clients of Gail and Connie's. Ironically, five years earlier they had been on opposite sides of the courtroom when Gail had been called upon by her firm to defend Damon Powell against charges that he had brutally murdered Vivian Seymour, Floyd and Nancy's only child. Damon had been acquitted of the crime, and they all had moved on. Vivian's murder had never been solved, but Damon had proven himself worthy of the acquittal, and the Seymours had never shown any further resentment or suspicion of him. Now, with this new crime, and the possibility of new charges being brought against Damon, the Seymours would be subjected to all the doubts and uncertainty surrounding their daughter's death, not to mention the inevitable dredging up of old wounds and sorrows. Charles, as their nephew, would be hard put to keep an unbiased position during the difficult days ahead. He knew it, and Hugo knew it. There was not much else to be said.

Hugo moved the car expertly in and out of traffic the half-dozen miles along the parkway toward the city proper. Then it was another fifteen minutes or so outside of town to the suburban estate of the Seymours. Floyd Seymour was one of the more successful entrepreneurs of Cathcart, and his Long Hills home reflected it.

As Hugo wheeled to a stop in front of the large comfortable house, a figure darted out with an umbrella. 'Hi, Peter,' he said. 'I don't think we'll need that, but you can take Charles's things in if you like.'

'Yes, sir, Mr. Hugo. Family's in the living room. Come right on in. I'll take care of all this for you.'

Charles retrieved something from his briefcase, then clapped the elderly man on the shoulder. 'Good to see you, Peter. Everyone in there all right?'

'Yes, sir. They're as all right as they can be, under the circumstance.'

A brief cloud passed over the old man's face. He had been in service with the Seymours for a number of years. He still grieved with the rest of them over the tragic loss of Vivian, his golden-haired favorite.

Peter stood aside to allow the two men to enter ahead of him, taking their coats and waving them off to the waiting family before returning to the car to retrieve the bags. 'There's hot coffee brewing,' he called out over his shoulder. 'I'll bring it in as soon as I get these bags put away.'

'Thanks, Peter,' Charles said. 'That sounds wonderful.'

'Charles, good to see you. Did you have a decent trip?' Floyd Seymour turned away from the blazing fire and marched over to his nephew as the two men entered the room. Clapping him on the back, he embraced the younger man warmly. 'And Hugo. Thanks for bringing him out. Come on, you two. Have a seat by the fire. Peter will bring us some coffee, shortly — or would you rather have something stronger?' He motioned toward a well-stocked bar cart in the far corner of the well-appointed room.

Charles paused to bend over an older woman seated in a wing chair, her hands outstretched before the fire. 'How are you, Aunt Nancy? I hope this all isn't going to be hard on the two of you.' He kissed her forehead, noting with concern the deepened furrows and tell-tale traces of tears on her cheeks. 'Nothing too strong for me, Uncle Floyd,' he added, answering his uncle's question. Hugo put up a hand signaling 'no' as well, before taking a seat to one side. 'Oh Charles,' Nancy Seymour said. 'I don't know how I can bear it, going through … all this again. Please tell me it's some huge mistake. And that young girl, Marilyn Watson — is it true? Was she killed in the same — '

'Now, you know I'm not going to be able to talk to you about the case. That's why I suggested I stay at the hotel. I can't discuss anything with you while I'm providing support for Connie and Gail. And I truly understand how you feel, but you've got to understand what a delicate position I'm in, as well.' His words trailed off into a strained silence. Perhaps he should have ignored his uncle's wishes and gone straight to the hotel. He glanced at Hugo, who was maintaining a studied nonchalance. Charles could almost hear the unspoken 'I told you so.'

'Well, you can't blame us for feeling uncertain about this situation,' Floyd began. 'After all, the problem as I see it is that if Damon didn't kill Vivian, as you all seem to believe, then there's still a monster out there. Maybe still in our midst. If it wasn't Damon, then who could it have been?'

Charles didn't respond, but was surprised when Hugo spoke up. 'Sir, I know you probably don't believe it, but I can understand exactly how you feel. He shook his head as Floyd Seymour tried to interrupt him. 'Yes, I know it wasn't my daughter. But I've had colleagues ... friends ... in the business, who were injured badly, and in one case paid the ultimate price. And I was saddened and felt responsible for bringing the culprits to justice. I hate cold cases, and I'd do anything to solve this particular one. But Damon Powell was tried by a jury of his peers and cleared of that charge in a court of law. And I believe they got it right. I've worked with that young man for the last five years or so. I think I'm a pretty good judge of character at this point in my career, and I just don't believe he has it in him to be capable of killing someone. Particularly a senseless crime like the one that took your Vivian. Now, that's just my two cents, but for what it's worth, I think the killer is still out there ... and I don't think its Damon.'

Peter entered the room and began setting up the coffee service on a white-clothed table in the corner. When all was ready, he began pouring, serving Nancy Seymour first at her chair, then helping the others as they made their way over to the improvised station. 'Sally's made some sandwiches as well, ma'am,' he said as he helped Nancy. Shall I bring them in?'

'That would be fine. I'm sure Charles and Hugo must be hungry.'

Peter turned and left the room, returning a few minutes later with a tray of sandwiches that soon fell prey to the hungry duo.

Charles began to relax a little, and feel more at home. Of course the Seymours were upset by this reopening of old wounds. It was up to him to find the right way to discuss the situation with them, without violating any privilege in regards to the firm. They were his family, after all. Connie and Gail would both be well aware of his position and the delicate path he would have to tread. Knowing that, they had still asked him to come and help during this emergency. They must be confident that he would be capable of maintaining a proper balance.

He caught Hugo's eye, and nodded as the detective rose to make his departure. Hugo was a good friend. As were Connie and Gail. He had great friends, and family who cared about him. He was sitting in front of a warm fire, with a perfect cup of coffee.

For right this moment, all was right with the world.

*   *   *

Dinner at the Seymours' that evening was an uncomfortable affair. Normally, Charles Walton enjoyed his aunt and uncle's company, and the dinner-table conversation was pleasant and stimulating. Nancy Seymour kept an impeccable kitchen, and the tasty food was ladled out in substantial proportions. No one ever left her table unsatisfied.

Uncle Floyd was a self-made entrepreneur who, in spite of early fits and starts, had carved out a remarkable empire for his family and friends in the mid-sized town of Cathcart. He enjoyed regaling his companions with endless stories of deals and trades in which he was always the hero, coming out ahead of the game through natural wit and market-savvy honed by years of experience. Charles was always amused by these tales of derring-do, and kept up a challenging banter designed to both charm his uncle and goad him on to grander expositions. He suspected Floyd knew this, but it was a good-natured game they played, and no harm was done.

This evening, however, felt different. Aunt Nancy seemed distracted and out of sorts. There was an early calamity in the kitchen that produced an inedible first course. Then a dropped serving dish spoiled part of the main course. No amount of murmurings about 'It tastes just fine' and 'The roast is perfect on its own without the potatoes' could save the meal. And when the dessert soufflé, his aunt's specialty, fell flatter than a pancake, Floyd took the cue and suggested he and Charles retire to the den for brandy and cigars.

'Are you sure I can't help clean up?' Charles offered lamely, but Nancy shooed them away, saying it would be easier if she just did it herself.

'I know where everything goes, and I have Sally to help,' she said firmly. 'I know you're tired from the trip, and I'd really rather you and Floyd go smoke your cigars and get out of my hair.' She gave him a little shove and a half-smile to show she was trying to joke about it. He had no choice but to follow her orders.

In the den, Floyd's domain, the two men settled down in a couple of overstuffed chairs, and Charles relaxed a bit. Floyd swished his brandy around in the snifter before taking a sip.

'Now, Charles — tell me just what Gail and Connie are expecting you to do while you're here. Somewhat a presumption, I think, them calling you away from your legitimate work to help them defend that … that young man.'

Charles paused to light his cigar before answering. 'It's not like that at all, Floyd. They always have a full agenda, you know that. They're the most successful firm in Cathcart right now, but that means they give full service to each and every one of their clients, just as they do for you. What I'll be doing is keeping up with their regular clients — including you, of course. That'll free them up to handle this new issue. That's all.'

The firm of Osterwitz and Brevard was counsel to Seymour Enterprises, which included the town's largest shopping mall. Floyd knew full well that his business alone took up a huge segment of the firm's time. Add in a dozen other large clients throughout the area on retainer, not to mention new cases coming in all the time, plus the inevitable pro bono work for the local Bar Association, and it was obvious how careful

Charles's colleagues had to be just to stay on top of everything.

'Now they have this sudden … ' Charles paused. Had to be delicate here, ' … new situation confronting one of their staff. You know they're duty-bound to defend him, Floyd. I have a sense of what you're thinking, but you must understand they feel they have a moral obligation to step up for Damon.' There. He'd said the name they had both been trying to avoid.

Floyd, being a practical man, had not allowed his mixed feelings about the young man's previous trial and verdict to prevent him from using the services of the acknowledged best legal firm in town, the newly formed team of Conrad Osterwitz and Gail Brevard. Nancy, seemingly, had recovered as well, keeping busy with community and volunteer projects, and even helping out from time to time with the design aspects of her husband's shopping center. And Charles, the Seymours' nephew, had over time become a good friend and colleague of Gail and Connie's. Enough so, that when the position of full partner, with responsibility for their firm's Arizona office, was offered to him, he did not hesitate to accept the position.

But now Damon Powell was under arrest again, for a crime very similar to the earlier one — and just as horrifying. And there was one huge truth hovering in the haze of cigar smoke which neither man had dared to mention yet.

Vivian Seymour's murderer had never been apprehended. There was still a monster out there, roaming around free, who had savagely taken their precious girl from them. And now, it appeared, the killer had struck again.

*　*　*

In the middle of the night, as he tossed and turned in the unfamiliar bed, Charles's thoughts took an uncomfortable turn. Was it really ethical for him to be so closely aligned with the people who were determined, at all costs, to defend Damon Powell? After all the torment his family had been through following the vicious murder of his young cousin, where did his loyalty really lie?

Aunt Nancy had been close to a

breakdown after enduring the first trial and its unsettling outcome. She was bed-ridden for days, followed by weeks of despair, crying fits and even threats of suicide. Gradually, with the loving care of family and friends, she had recovered — at least on the surface. But Charles knew, after looking into her sad, tear-filled eyes this evening, that she was very close to the brink again with this new threat.

Could he, in good conscience, turn away from his own flesh and blood in order to help defend a man he didn't know that well? A man who could still, quite possibly, be the real murderer? The longer he thought about it, the more uncertain he became.

Charles Walton did not sleep well that night. And he was not alone.

9

Hal Watson struggled on through the snow-filled ruts of the narrow roadway. At each turn he paused to look about, straining to see through the ever-darkening mist, searching for anything that might provide shelter. He continued to rub his left shoulder, where the discomfort seemed to be growing worse. He tried not to dwell on the possibility that he was suffering some sort of attack. A heart attack? The idea kept creeping back into his mind. *No*, he told himself, *it's just a pulled muscle. I'm sure of it. I did something to it scrambling out of that car. It can't be anything other than that.*

His breath came in short pants, visible steam rising into the air with each gasp. The cold was crippling. Wearing only street clothes and slick-soled shoes, he was at a distinct disadvantage. Only a fool would venture out into this weather dressed as he was … and Hal Watson was no fool.

He almost laughed at the sheer irony of it all. He should be at home right now, curled up with a hot drink in front of a blazing fire, perusing a favorite book or listening to a favorite bit of music. Marilyn would be safe at home with him, getting ready for her busy day tomorrow, clearing up a bit in the kitchen, or even sitting there with him talking over her current activities — her night out with Damon, their future together ...

He had to stop this. It would not get him through the next few hours. And he had to get through — survive somehow — to get back and tell his tale. The monster back in the car had to be discovered. The truth must come out.

Just as he thought he could go no further, and was prepared to slip down in the snow and rest ... fall asleep ... whatever, he spotted something just off the roadway.

You could easily miss it, if you weren't looking. It was a small, dark, rectangular shape, half-hidden by draping firs and cedars. The road was starting to curve in the opposite direction, which would distract anyone driving by away from it.

There was no clear path into the little clearing, but being on foot, Hal could see enough to make his way carefully through the trees towards it. He hoped it was a shelter of sorts. He was beginning to believe that, in spite of his miraculous escape from the wrecked car, he could easily die of exposure out here in a snowdrift. With the heavy snowfall covering all traces, his dead body would lie out here unnoticed for months, until spring thaws revealed his whereabouts. And even then, he realized, they might not find him in the shelter, if that was what it was, for long afterwards.

As he drew nearer to the darkened blob, he sobbed a sigh of relief. It was a cabin — small and humbly constructed, but definitely shelter, with a door and, he saw with jubilation, a small, sturdy chimney poking up through a cedar-shingled roof. If there was dry firewood in there, he would be able to start a fire!

He fingered the thin matchbook in his pocket. He was not a smoker, but he carried it always, just in case. Tonight, that silly little precaution might save his life. But how to get in?

He struggled up steep steps to a rough-hewn deck and made his way to the door. He tried the old-fashioned latch but, of course, it was locked tight. He thought a minute, then reached up and felt above the door jamb. Nothing.

Then he looked down. A small overhang shielded the doorway from the snow. In front of the door lay a thick sisal welcoming mat. He bent and pulled up the corner. There was the key.

Elated, he picked it up and grasped it tightly in his numb fingertips. Carefully, he directed it into the keyhole. He struggled to turn it. At first he thought it wouldn't work, but then gradually, so as not to break it off, he moved it back and forth, until, miracle of miracles, it turned. Saying a little prayer, he took hold of the knob and opened the door.

He lunged forward into the darkness, heaving a sigh of relief, not caring what was ahead. He fell to the floor and lay in a heap for a little bit, trying to still his pounding heart and ignore the ache in his shoulder, and trying to find enough strength to make the last effort to save himself.

Finally, after a few minutes, he recovered enough to get up and take stock of his surroundings. There was no light, of course, and the few windows were all heavily shuttered. At first he stumbled and hit against various objects until he had enough sense to stand still and let his eyes adjust as much as possible to the dim surroundings. Night had not yet fallen completely, and the bit of ambient light creeping in from the open doorway allowed him to begin to make out the interior of the room. Eventually, he could see the outlines of a small stone fireplace set into one of the side walls. He moved toward it, hands outstretched to encounter any obstacles in his way. He stopped in front of the hearth and took stock.

Immediately to the right was a metal stand holding several long-handled tools. To the left was a large bin. Hoping the miracle would continue, he felt about for the mouth of the bin, then reached down inside. His groping fingers touched something solid and angular. He grabbed hold and pulled it up and out. A small log! With luck, he could get a fire going — and then all things would be possible.

He needed a starter; paper of some kind. He pulled out the small diary-sized notebook he always carried and began ripping the pages out, one by one, then crumpling them up. He did not care what he was tearing up, or what messages or stray phone numbers he was destroying. What did any of that matter now?

Finally, he had a small pile of crumpled up paper. Tinder? He reached back into the bin and was rewarded with a small bundle of fir limbs, needles still attached. They appeared to be dry enough to serve. He pulled out his precious matches — couldn't waste any of these; he must make sure he got the fire set and going strong with just one or two. He picked up the log and laid it gently on the grate, tucked the fir kindling in and around it, then nestled the little bundle of crumpled-up paper deep down in the midst of it all.

Taking a deep breath, he took one match from the book and struck it on the firing strip. Once, twice, he struck without luck. Maybe he had carried these around too long. What if, after all this effort, he could not get the match to strike?

One more time. He held the book firmly in his left hand, and just as firmly pulled the edge of the match along the strip with his right. It lit!

Smoothly, so as not to blow out the smoldering tip, he held it, hand trembling, to the paper cone. At first nothing happened. Then, as if touched by an angel, the flame of the match grew in strength and became one with the paper. Then the paper caught fire and blossomed like an orange-red flower in the darkened stone cavern of the fire pit.

Taking one of the metal fire tools from its stand, Hal carefully began introducing the tips of the fir branches to the merry little imp of a flame. At first he despaired of getting the branches to pick up the bits of fire and clasp them to their limbs. He had no trouble doing this, getting his own fireplace to perform, when he was safe at home. But this situation was different. So much more depended on it.

Still, his luck held. One by one, the needles on the twigs, then the limbs themselves, began to burn with vigor. The room began to lighten up a bit. Things seemed a bit cheerier. But would the log take? That was the big 'if.' He wondered if there was another log, or more, hidden away in that bin. He didn't dare turn his attention away from the fledgling fire to look, but he began to worry about how he would keep the fire going without fuel. Was there a chair or a table in here? Did he have the strength to take them apart to use as firewood?

He watched and waited, prodding here and there around the perimeter of the little fire, trying to direct the searching fingers of flame toward the mighty meal of a log sitting right there in its midst, just waiting for the fire to devour it.

Hal continued to watch anxiously, as first one and then another of the kindling twigs in the rough stone fireplace caught fire. If only the solid log would catch!

At last he felt comfortable enough to glance about the tiny room. His eyes had adjusted to the dim light cast by the tiny flames, and he looked for anything that might be of use to him. As soon as he was confident he could leave the fire unattended, he made his way back to the wood bin and removed the lid altogether. He could see a stack of good-sized logs resting in the bottom, and he had already spotted two spindly chairs he thought he could break apart as well. So firewood was taken care of, at least for the moment. Then he saw a large box of wooden kitchen matches perched conspicuously on the rough-hewn fireplace mantle, so he need not have worried about his own short supply of fire-starters.

A makeshift counter of sorts had been set up at the back of the room, and there was a small tin pie safe resting on it. Opening it up, he was elated to see several rows of canned beans, soup and the like. More than enough to keep him nourished for a while. He could probably eke out a week's worth of meals, if he was careful. On the far wall, a camp cot made up with heavy quilts and blankets promised a warm place to sleep. So far, so good.

He began to rummage around for any-thing else that would be useful, and pulled out a compact first aid kit. Some odds and ends of clothing and a heavy parka hung from pegs on the wall, and nearby was a pair of ancient galoshes that looked roomy enough to fit him. He had been hoping against hope for something like a shortwave radio set-up, or even a phone of some kind, but found nothing that might provide a means of communication with the outside world. Too much to expect, he supposed.

His own cell phone had been left behind at the house in the panic and urgency of his forced withdrawal. There might not be service this far out in any case. Still, he wished he had had the presence of mind to thrust it in his pocket at the last moment. His abductor might not have noticed, and it was always possible he could have gotten an emergency call out before they were too far out of town, in time for someone to find and rescue him.

He sighed again, realizing that therein lay his dilemma. No one knew where he was. Probably no one was even aware he was missing. Unless, or until, the mess back at the house was discovered, no one would know anything was wrong. He was due in court tomorrow, and if he didn't show up he felt sure his secretary would go out to the house to find out why. She had a key, and no doubt she would be the one to discover what had happened there, and that he was now missing.

But he had no idea how long this storm might last; and if the snowpack ended up as deep as he feared, there would be no way he could fight his way back down that long trail to civilization. Nor would there be any tracks remaining to point the way to his location.

He tried to recollect how many miles he had driven before the accident, but drew a complete blank. He had been more concerned about the individual in the back seat than judging how far they had come.

And then, too, there was the issue of the continuing dull ache in his left arm and shoulder. He kept telling himself he had merely strained a muscle, either getting out of the car or struggling up that blasted hillside. But he was well aware of the other, more serious possibility.

It would do him no good to make the effort to walk out of here, only to die along the way of a severe heart attack. No. He was stuck here for the long haul. And that thought frightened the hell out of him. He

102

had thought he was resigned to his fate. After all, he had nothing left to live for now, did he? But somehow the urge to survive was still burning in his soul.

He pulled out a second log and placed it near the fire, ready to re-stoke the blaze when necessary. Then he stripped off his wet shirt, pants, shoes and socks, and stretched them over one of the rickety chairs near the fire to dry. He sorted through the mish-mash of clothing until he found a roomy pair of sweat pants, a long-sleeved woolen shirt and heavy knit socks that, thankfully, fit him well enough. He drew them on, not caring if they were soiled or musty. What difference did the niceties make now?

Some short time later, Hal Watson was seated before a roaring fire in the most comfortable chair, wrapped in a blanket, watching beans heat up in a little kettle on a hook over the open flame. A tin cup of melting snow gleaned from the front stoop sat on the stone hearth. He had found teabags as well, and was surprised to realize he was anticipating the little improvised meal to come with something akin to elation.

He sat gazing into the fire, trying to reason through his predicament. His legal training was useful to him now. He had spent many an hour talking a client through some disastrous calamity or other, getting them to see the advantage of remaining calm, and looking — always looking — for the best way forward. Now he must do the same for himself.

As the beans bubbled away over the fire, he began to feel a little more optimistic. At least he wasn't going to die of exposure out in the storm tonight. With any luck, he would find his way back home eventually. Then there would be all hell to pay for the individual who had landed him in this situation.

10

Damon Powell had assured Gail and Hugo that he was perfectly all right to return to his apartment and spend the night there alone. Both had offered to put him up as long as he needed, or to take him out to his parents' house, but he had steadfastly refused. He was comfortable in his own place, he had all his things there, and quite frankly he didn't want any company.

Finally, assured that he had plenty of food on hand and would be all right for the night at least, Hugo and Gail waved good-bye and drove off towards the Community Hospital to see about Erle. Damon would be able to pick up his own car at the firm's parking facility the next day. He had no idea if he was permitted to drive, under the conditions of the bail bond, but he would find all that out tomorrow. Right now, all he wanted was a little peace and quiet to lick his wounds, and time to sort out all the horrible events of the day.

Gingerly, he removed his clothing and took a steaming hot shower. He examined the emerging bruises on his midsection and decided the ribs weren't broken. The black-and-blue patches would heal in time, so he guessed he was none the worse for wear.

He got into pajamas, robe and slippers and lit the gas fireplace in the comfortable, if small, living area. He put a kettle on to boil and rummaged around for teabags. He didn't drink hot tea often, but it sounded like just the thing right now.

As soon as he was settled in an easy chair in front of the fire, he began reviewing all the events of the prior evening, sipping at the tea from time to time, and making notes on a legal pad with the Parker fountain pen from the 1920s which had been a treasured gift from Marilyn on his last birthday.

OK, starting with dinner. They had agreed to go to the Napoli because Damon liked their choices of individual pizzas, and Mari said she loved their large fresh salads. Neither of them wanted a heavy dinner, and the Napoli, unlike some of the other dinner houses, didn't close after lunch service, so they could dine as early as they wished.

True to form, Damon had ordered his favorite Pizza Marguerita, and Mari settled for the avocado-bacon salad with swiss cheese. He had iced tea and she had a diet soda. Silly; she was always worried about her weight. He thought she was perfect just as she was.

Resolutely blinking back the tears coming unbidden into his staring eyes, Damon continued his list.

What exactly *had* they talked about? Marilyn was concerned about a paper she had to complete within the next week for a class on torts. He'd given her some advice about the ins and outs of tort law, which he had studied the previous term, and they agreed on the approach she would take with her essay.

He had commented on his own struggle with the concept of habeus corpus, its definition and use. 'If it's so easy,' he said, 'why isn't it used more frequently?'

'I think it's considered a petition of last resort.' Marilyn paused to spear a bright green chunk of avocado. 'I think the court considers it useful only when all other avenues have failed.'

'Hmm. I suppose you're right about that.'

They were comfortably silent for a minute before she spoke again. 'I had the strangest feeling today.' She stopped eating for a second and took a sip of her drink. 'I almost thought I was being followed. Everywhere I went, I felt like eyes were on me. Very creepy.'

Damon's heart froze. He had completely forgotten that part of the conversation. Not until he had gone back through everything they talked about, did he remember this one crucial bit. He wrote the words down, those damning words, in the ink flowing from one of the last gifts she had given him. He had the distinct feeling that there was truth in that statement. What if the killer had actually been stalking her throughout the day? Would there be a record of it somewhere? Were there CRT surveillance monitors in and around the areas Marilyn had visited yesterday?

Convinced he was onto a lead, Damon grabbed his cell phone and quickly texted Hugo. *Call me asap. I remember something.*

Within a few minutes, his phone sang out and he grabbed it. 'Hugo? I just remembered something critical. I think Marilyn may have been stalked by her assailant. This is what I remember …'

As soon as Damon stopped speaking, Hugo responded. 'That's great, Damon. You've just hit upon one of the first rules of detection: Go over everything again and again. Eventually, your subconscious kicks in and you can remember details you never thought you would. I've seen this time and time again with witnesses. Sometimes even the simplest thing will trigger a memory just beneath the surface. Keep up the good work. In the meantime, I'll start reviewing any and all cameras in and around Hal's office. I'll start interviewing people in the area — shops, lunch places. You never know what you'll turn up.'

After he hung up, Damon took another sip of tea and looked back down at his notes. He had covered a whole page, and he was only through the first part of their dinner. This was going to take longer than he thought.

11

'Good morning, Mr. Walton. It's good to see you again. They're all in Ms. Brevard's office. Go right on in.'

'Thanks, June,' Charles smiled at the office manager. 'Good to see you, too.'

He went through the double doors and down the hall until he reached the entry to Gail's office, and hesitated. Normally he would walk right in, expecting a warm welcome from his friends. But this morning felt different somehow. He heard a murmur of voices from within, and knocked.

'Come in,' a voice he recognized as Connie's responded.

He opened the door and entered. There was a brief uncomfortable moment as he stepped inside and paused, then the murmuring continued. Gail was seated at her desk, carrying on what appeared to be an involved phone conversation. She waved at him, all the while nodding vigorously as she kept up her side of the conversation.

'Of course, Ralph. I understand what you're saying. But you have nothing to be concerned about.' There was a crackle on the other end of the phone and Gail nodded again. 'Yes, but that's just it. I'd rather have someone available to assist us right now, and I assure you — ' The phone crackled again. 'Look, Ralph, he's just come in. Are you free later on today? What about lunch? I can't join you, but I'm sure he'll be available.' She glanced at Charles with a question on her face. He nodded. 'Yes, he's available. What about one p.m. or so at Waterfords? I'll call right now and make the reservation. I'll give him the file, if that's all right with you.' The phone erupted again. 'All right, one at Waterfords. It's on us. No, I insist. All right.'

She rang off and heaved a sigh of relief. 'Sorry, Charles, but I'm going to have to throw you to the wolves — or should I say wolf, in the person of Ralph Del Monaco. You've heard of him?'

Charles nodded and moved to the chair on the other side of her desk, placing his worn leather briefcase on the floor beside him. 'Yeah. I remember the old man, at least — Nino? What's the case about?'

'Not that complicated. Nino Del Monaco passed away last March. Nothing unexpected about that; he was 97, I think, and had been in poor health for the last few years. Problem is, every shirt-tail relative in the world has now surfaced to demand a piece of the pie.'

Charles grimaced. Nothing like greedy relatives to pick over the poor man's remains.

'Anyway,' Gail continued, 'Ralph, his oldest grandson, is the rightful heir to the Del Monaco estate and enterprises. Most of the other claims are spurious, if not completely outrageous. But we still have to go through all the motions. You know the drill. Ralph's a bit gun-shy at this point, and was not happy when I suggested allowing you to handle some of these court appearances for me while we deal with Damon's defense. He's actually a pretty decent guy, though, and I'm sure he'll come around once he meets you and feels more comfortable. As you just heard, I've arranged for you to have lunch with him today. I'll give you the files so you can get an idea of what's required. I think the next court date is Thursday.

That should give you a few days to review everything we've done so far.'

Charles nodded. 'Of course. Give me the file and I'll look through it. If I have any questions I'll let you know, but it sounds pretty straightforward to me. You know I cut my teeth on this sort of thing.'

He wasn't particularly happy about all this, but he owed a great deal to Connie and Gail. If he could help in any way right now, it would go a long way towards repaying their generosity to him in the past. He managed a grin, and she smiled back.

'Thanks, Charles. You're a lifesaver right now. This other thing is … ' She hesitated, suddenly remembering Charles's relationship to the Seymours. 'Oh my God,' she said softly. 'Charles, I'm so sorry. I didn't mean to be cavalier about the situation. This must be very difficult for you. Perhaps we shouldn't have asked … '

'Nonsense, Gail. We're a team. At least that's way I view it. If I can't pull my weight in times like this, then I'm no good to anyone, especially myself. I'll do everything I possibly can to fill the void for you.' He stopped short, considering his position. 'Of course, I do believe it'd be somewhat of a conflict of interest for me to get too involved in Damon's defense,' he went on. 'Floyd and Nancy ... well, they're very upset about this new atrocity, to put it mildly. I'm going to have to tread a very fine line here. I think it'd be better if I don't discuss the Powell case with you any more than necessary. I don't want to put you in a bad position, and I certainly don't want my aunt and uncle worrying about all the gory details, either. I'm sure you all understand.'

He realized, suddenly, that he had raised his voice. Looking around, he saw Hugo at a corner table. The detective had been discussing something earnestly with one of his operatives. Connie was seated on a sofa in the conversation area, pen in hand, and yellow pads piled high around him. Both had looked up when he began speaking, and waited patiently until he was through.

'Hi, Charles. Good to see you,' said Connie. 'Why don't you grab a cup of coffee and let's talk this thing through.' He gestured toward the refreshment bar in the corner.

'Hi, Connie. And good, as always, to see you.' He nodded at Hugo, who returned to instructing his employee.

'The way I see it,' Connie went on, 'we're very fortunate to have you as one of our professional team. And we *are* a team. We all understand how very difficult it is for you to come back here under these circumstances. I can't tell you how grateful we are that you've been willing to do so.'

Charles started to say something, but Connie shook his head. 'You're here because you chose to do something difficult in order to help out your friends. That's the only way we can look at this. So here's my take on it. Right now, we're committed to Damon's defense. If anything changes in that regard, believe me, you'll be the first to know. In the meantime, we've got a pretty busy practice here, with lots of ongoing cases that require a seasoned attorney of high caliber to shepherd them through the process.

'Both Gail and I have several court appearances scheduled and, frankly, I just don't think we can handle both responsibilities. If you're willing to help us take up the slack, watchdog our ongoing cases and help plan and reschedule some of the lesser projects, we'd be very grateful. If you feel you can't in good conscience divide your loyalties between family and friends, we won't think any the less of you because of it.' It was a long speech for Connie. He sat back on the couch to await Charles's answer.

Charles stared out the window at the dark sky. The initial storm had passed, but all the clouds were still there. Finally he bestirred himself, rose and walked over to the bar and poured a cup of coffee. Returning to the corner of Gail's desk, he sat and stretched out a hand. 'Well, young lady, where are those Del Monaco files? I need to get busy if I'm going to meet this Ralph for lunch.'

'Thanks, Charles,' said Connie from the sofa. 'I knew we could count on you. This will never be forgotten.'

'Ah, shucks, boss,' said Charles with a grin. 'I never could resist a challenge.'

★　★　★

'All right,' Hugo said, 'let's start from the beginning.'

It was later the same day, and Hugo had arranged to drive Damon's car back to the apartment for him. At the same time, he requested an in-depth interview to clarify some of the facts in the case, especially Damon's movements on the day of the attack.

Damon Powell took a deep breath and plunged in. 'I got up at about six, I guess. I usually get up about that time, and don't even set the clock, unless I have an early appointment I can't miss. I showered, shaved, dressed and had a light breakfast before leaving the apartment to drive to school.'

'Did you call anyone, or talk to anyone at all, before you left the apartment, or on your way to class?'

'No. Er, that's not exactly true — I exchanged a few words with Jason Kimball. He lives in the apartment across the hall from me, and we often leave here about the same time in the morning. We rode down to the parking structure in the elevator together.'

'What did you discuss? Did you say

anything to him about Marilyn?'

'God, no! I barely know the man; only to say hello in the elevator. He's a baseball freak, and he's always going on about last night's game. I don't care for baseball myself, so I usually just let him have his say, and nod or respond with something trivial. It's playoff season, you know, so he was probably talking about his favorite team … the Cubs, I think.'

'But he'd remember seeing you in the elevator? Talking to you?'

'Oh yeah, I'm sure he would … well, maybe. Like I said, it wasn't rocket science we were discussing.'

'Okay.'

Hugo was silent a minute as he jotted down a note or two about Jason Kimball as a possible witness for the defense. If this neighbor saw Damon calmly going about his normal day, at least at the beginning of it, it might add to the picture they were trying to paint of their client as helpless victim, not vicious murderer. 'Go on,' he said, sitting back and sipping his coffee. The more laid-back he seemed to be, the more relaxed Damon would be in talking about his activities on the day in question. This was a common tactic Hugo employed when gathering evidence. Put the witness at ease. They will always be more cooperative and responsive.

'There's really not much to tell. I drove out to the campus and got there at about eight, parked, and walked in to the law building. My first class was at ten, but I like to get on campus early, get in, get settled, and maybe do some preliminary prep before class actually starts.'

'Again, did anyone see you when you arrived on campus, someone who would remember you?'

'No, I don't think … ' Damon stopped and screwed up his face in thought. This was so difficult, trying to remember each and every little detail about that day. If he had known what a difference it would make, he would have made a note of everything. Trying to recall in retrospect each significant event was damn near impossible.

'Wait. I remember now. I *didn't* go directly to the law building. I stopped off at the library to return some books. I was early enough that I went ahead and sat down in there awhile to go over my notes for class. The prof has a habit of giving pop quizzes without advance notice, so I like to be prepared for that. I just reviewed everything we were supposed to have read for this particular class, trying to be as prepared as possible.'

'But did anyone see you — anyone who would remember — '

'That's what I was getting to. Yes — there's a guy in one of my study groups, the one on dispute resolution. He came up to me in the library and asked if I remembered what night we were going to meet this coming week. He'd missed the previous meeting and we'd changed the dates because too many people had conflicts.'

'What's his name?'

'God … let's see. I'm drawing a blank. I can find out, though. He's in my class. The instructor would know if I can't remember. Let me come back to that.'

'Okay, that's good. Did you talk to him very long? Discuss anything other than your classes?'

'No. He just wanted to know about the time and date of the next get-together. I looked it up on my date log and gave it to him. We exchanged pleasantries, that's all. I don't think I talked to him more than five minutes or so. But I'm pretty sure he'd remember, because of the date thing.'

'So, then you went to class? And, of course, you'd be logged in there as being in attendance?'

'Yes. I was even called on to make a bit of a presentation. I'm sure the instructor would remember that, as well as most of the other students. The truth is, I flubbed it a bit, and we all laughed about it. I made a little joke about not being as well prepared as I thought. Too smug, you know. Everyone laughed, including the professor.'

'Good. Sounds like you seemed comfortable; at ease with yourself and the situation.'

'Honestly, I have no idea how I came across. I was angry with myself, especially since I *had* studied the material. It was just a minor goof, but the whole thing made me feel like a fool.'

'It's okay. Anything to help present you as a normal human being, with nothing else on your mind that day but passing that course.'

Hugo paused again, adding a few more notes to the growing chronology of Damon's Day of Reckoning.

'Did you go off campus for lunch? Maybe meet Marilyn or someone else in town?'

'No, I didn't want to leave campus. Too much hassle. Marilyn's schedule was pretty hectic too. She had one class that day, but it was through the noon hour, so there was no way we could meet up easily. Instead, I just hiked over to the cafeteria and grabbed a quick bite … whatever their special was that day. Wait.' He pulled out his wallet and perused a few receipts before selecting one and presenting it to Hugo. 'Here's my receipt for lunch at the campus cafeteria. See, it has the date and time stamped on it.'

Hugo duly entered this information on his log and tucked the receipt away for safekeeping. 'How long were you in the cafeteria? And again, did anyone else see you there?'

'I said hi to a few of the students I know. I'm not sure which ones. I'll try to give that some thought, too, and come up with their names. I think I was there about half an hour to 45 minutes at least. I know I went in about a quarter after eleven, after my first class finished. I suppose I was back in the library by noon. My second class didn't start until one, but it was a two-hour class, lecture and lab.'

'Your professor and the students in that second class would remember seeing you there?'

'Oh, sure. Especially for the lab part. We had to do some practice trial work with partners. I can get you all those names as well. I suppose we were done a little after three o'clock, I took my time walking back to the parking structure, picked up my car ... Oh yes, I should have my parking ticket for the day, too.' He paused while he rummaged through his receipts again. 'Yes, here it is. Just as I thought — it shows I parked in the structure at five past eight and didn't retrieve my car until ten past three. Here.'

Hugo carefully smoothed out the receipt, wrote down the times as recorded, and placed the bit of paper lovingly in the evidence pouch clipped inside his notebook. 'This is all very good. It's establishing a normal day for you. If I can find some of these students and professors who'd be willing to confirm your whereabouts and state of mind throughout the day, it should go a long way toward providing a positive picture of your attitude and frame of mind.' He paused again. 'Now for the hard part. I need to know everything that happened and everything you thought and saw for the next few hours of that day. Are you up for this?'

Damon grimaced. This was the part he was dreading; the part he now had to relive. The last hours of Marilyn Walton's life. And the last happy hours of his own existence.

He retrieved his own pad of notes, the ones he had written out so carefully last night, in his treasured fountain pen's ink; ink as black as the depths of his soul. As black, perhaps, as the dried blood at a crime scene.

'I'm ready,' he said. 'Let's get this part of it over with.'

12

True to her promise, Lucy Verner arrived at the Norris home in the middle of the afternoon.

'Nonsense!' she had said in response to Connie's offer to drive her down from her upstate home. 'I'm perfectly capable of driving down there, and I prefer my own car to that behemoth of Alberta's.' She was referring to the old classic Cadillac that Alberta Norris still drove to the grocery store and doctor's appointments. 'Besides, who knows — we might need two cars while I'm there. Better be prepared for any eventuality, that's my motto!'

Connie thanked her, but urged her to let him know immediately if she had any problem at all with planning for the trip. 'Money?' he queried. 'I can give you a credit card number to use for any emergency. I have one put aside for you to use while you're here.'

'Poppycock!' Lucy erupted. 'You'll do

nothing of the kind. Alberta's like a sister to me. There's only the two of us left now, and I suppose between the two of us, we can cover anything that comes up. We'll let you know if that changes. But for now, it'd be just one more thing to worry about.'

'Well,' he said, a smile touching his lips, 'I sure appreciate that, Lucy. But Gail and I want you to know how very grateful we are for you stepping in like this. We're going to try and get this whole situation resolved as soon as possible. But frankly, we're very concerned about the both of them.'

'I know,' Lucy said. She paused. 'Alberta's done everything she can to make that boy's life as good as it can be. I don't know how anyone could've done more. But she's run out of steam now. I could tell that the last time we talked. I should've come right down there then. But I didn't.

'Now I need to make up for that. I've put my house in mothballs, so to speak. I have several friends and neighbors who'll make certain everything's all right there. I've stopped my newspaper, and I've arranged for my mail to be forwarded. I've got two suitcases packed in my car, and a tank full of gas. I've got my attitude in place, and my work clothes at the ready. I'm in for the long haul, Connie. You can count on me.'

'Thank you, Lucy. You're an answer to our prayers. As I said, we're committed to getting all this resolved in the best way for everyone, just as quickly as we possibly can. But in the meantime … well, just thank you, my dear. You're just what the doctor ordered.'

'Okey-dokey, then. I'm on my way. And don't you worry about a thing. Alberta and I will do just fine.'

★ ★ ★

Erle was not happy. After the first excitement of the ride home with Hugo, followed by Mother fussing over him, hot chocolate in front of the fire, and all the attention, reality had set in.

'Erle,' Gail said to him with that funny, unhappy noise her voice made when she was talking to him about something he shouldn't have done, 'I want you to try and remember why you decided to play such a naughty trick on Mother.'

He stamped his foot and crossed his arms, lips pouting. 'No. I don't have to tell you nothin' at all, Gail. You don't care 'bout me, anyhow. You never come to see me no more. Not ever!' He stamped his foot again in emphasis.

Gail was seated at the large table that served as desk and crafts station in Erle's brightly decorated suite of rooms. They were in the playroom, which opened onto the comfortable adjoining bedroom and bath. She took a different tack. 'Mother was very upset when she couldn't find you,' she began.

'NO! NO! NO!' screamed Erle, putting his fingers in his ears. 'I CAN'T HEAR YOU!'

'Very well,' Gail said quietly. 'I'll go away and leave you alone to think about all this. When you're ready to talk about it in your 'inside' voice, I'll come back and listen to what you have to tell me.' She got up, shoved her chair back under the table and turned to walk out the door. As she suspected, Erle ran up and grabbed her hand.

'No, Gail,' he pleaded. 'Sorry! I'm sorry! Don't go away. Please don't go!'

'All right,' she said. She took hold of his hand and patted it softly. 'All right. Let's go sit down and try again. I just want to help. If there's something wrong, it'd be better if you told me about it.'

Erle screwed up his face, and great fat tears tumbled down his cheeks. 'Yes. I want to tell you. I've been a bad boy … I want to tell you … '

'Tell me what, Erle? I don't think you're a bad boy at all. But we all make mistakes. If you made a mistake, you must tell me about it so I can help you fix it, and make it all better.'

He groaned. 'Very bad boy!'

'What did you do that was so very bad, Erle?'

'I'm not supposed to tell. But it's okay if I tell you, isn't it, Gail?'

'Yes, it's okay to tell me. I won't hurt you, you know that. And if you're in trouble, I can help make it better for you.'

He snuffled into the big white handkerchief she handed him and sat down across from her at his work table. 'Well,

129

it's about the game,' he began.

'Wait a minute. What game are you talking about? Whose game?'

'That's the part I can't tell. She said if I tell, something really bad will happen. Someone's going to get hurt really bad if I tell.'

He threw his head into his hands and burst into sobs once more. And this time, nothing Gail could say or do convinced him that it really was okay to tell her what he had done that was so very bad.

13

Hal Watson woke with a start. The wind outside the tiny cabin was moaning, hail peppered the roof, and a stray branch was scraping against the porch rail. The noise gave him the jitters. What if the monster in the car had recovered consciousness and had struggled, just as he had, up the snow-filled gorge to the road at the top? What if, right now, the creature stood, spare key in hand, poised to push open the door and invade this tiny haven of comfort and safety Hal had created for himself? What would he do?

Quickly, mindless of the continuing un-comfortable pressure in his chest, Hal threw off the covers and rose from the cot. He felt around under the thin padding that served as a mattress for the loaded pistol he had hidden there. For a moment, panic-stricken, he thought it was gone. He stared wildly at the flickering shadows in the corners of his cell, made huge by reflections from the embers in the still-smoldering fire. Perhaps his enemy had already broken in, had deduced where the weapon might be hidden, and had commandeered it while he slept.

Then he relaxed. His fingers closed around the icy steel barrel, and he pulled it forth and cradled it in his grasp. At least he still had this bit of security, this last-ditch defense against the evil outside.

Edgy now, and no longer drowsy, Hal made his way to the chair by the fireplace. He was still dressed in the same clothing he had found at the beginning of his exile, although he was unsure of just how much time had elapsed. He squinted at his watch. It should still be running accurately, he thought. The hands appeared to be set at 4:15 — but was it a.m. or p.m.? He couldn't be sure if he had been here one night or two. Or was it more than that? How long had he slept, anyway? And if the storm was still going strong, how much snow and ice had piled up in the road out front? How would he ever be able to make his way back to civilization in that mess?

He put his face in his hands and tried to think. At some point, he would run out of the canned food. Water wasn't an issue; he could always melt the snow piled up on the porch as needed. There was a pretty good stash of firewood in the bin, and the miscellaneous spindly chairs and tables would be a further source.

How long did these storms last? He wished he had paid more attention to such things. Weather and sports statistics had always taken a back seat to his legal studies when he was a kid. As he grew older, his actual cases took up most of his time. His favorite reading materials were mysteries. He had a great collection of Raymond Chandler, Rex Stout, Ross Macdonald and Dashiell Hammett classics on the bookshelf near his easy chair at home.

Home ... A stray tear traced a sad path down the furrow nearest his nose, and he brushed it away angrily. No time for such weakness. No time!

A call of nature forced him to his feet, and he shuffled in his sock feet across the tiny space to a curtained alcove he had discovered in his earlier investigations. It hid a chemical toilet of sorts. He had no idea how it functioned, but at least it gave him the option to … to … cover his tracks. He let out a hoot of laughter, then caught himself in alarm. Was he losing it? Was this what isolation did to people? He thought about the various clients in defense cases he had lost over the years. Was this how it felt to go to jail?

No, he decided. In jail, at least, there were other people around — guards, prisoners, the occasional visitor if one was fortunate. And at least you were assured of three square meals a day, minimal medical care (his hand made its way to the still-aching throb in his shoulder area), and a warm place to sleep.

No. In many ways this was worse than incarceration.

So how was he to escape? He returned to the warmth of the fire and set about preparing yet another cup of hot tea. Small pleasures.

Then on to deep thought. There had to be a way out of this prison. And he would have to find it.

14

Charles Walton stole another glance at his watch. 10:30. Fifteen minutes later than the last time he had looked, and still too early for lunch. And too late, really, for a mid-morning coffee break.

It wasn't that the neat pile of briefs he was reviewing on the desk in front of him was boring. There was enough variety and interest here to engage his attention. But he felt unsettled and antsy. Something kept niggling at the back of his brain; something he halfway recalled, and something intangible and annoying. What the hell was it? he thought in sudden exasperation.

He got up, stretched, and wandered over to the coffee service area, just as he had half a dozen times before. He looked over the offerings: herbal teas and flavored coffees, and a few pastries from early that morning that had been lying there far too long. He opened the under-counter fridge and removed a diet soda, sat down on the comfortable sofa in the visitor's area, and placed the soda can, unopened, on the coffee table.

He leaned back, sighed, and stared out the window behind the desk at the gray sky. A few flakes of snow were still drifting down. The weather had been relentless for the several days he had been here, but if the newscasters were correct, things were due to let up by the end of the week. He hoped so. The dark, dreary outlook was beginning to wear on him. He wished, in spite of his resolve, to be back in Phoenix, where it was still balmy even at this time of the year.

But more than that, he missed his friends, his colleagues, and his life there — the life he had created when he accepted Connie and Gail's offer of a partnership. He realized with a sudden pang how happy and satisfied he had become with his situation. He actually missed the home office in downtown Phoenix — his office, the one he had chosen and decorated to suit his taste; the one where he conducted business on his own terms, making all the decisions and living with the consequences of those decisions. Here, he was just another cog in the wheel, a piece of the puzzle. This was Connie and Gail's operation. And even though he was accorded every accommodation and treated by the staff with the respect due an acting partner in the organization, he felt somehow less important; less necessary.

He pounded his fist into the cushioned arm of the sofa. No! What a terrible attitude. He knew full well that his friends were counting on him to hold their practice together while they plowed full steam ahead into the murky mess that had become the Damon Powell case. He knew, beyond a shadow of a doubt, that they held him in high regard; considered him a crucial part of their team.

But that was just it, he was ashamed to admit to himself. He didn't want to be just a part of the team. He was much happier working on his own, handling his own cases, keeping his one-man business thriving in the town he had come to love and call home.

This town had once been his home. When both he and his cousin Nick had been orphaned at an early age, his aunt and uncle, the Seymours, had taken them in and given them everything they needed. Both boys were raised in the lap of luxury, at least as much luxury as the middle-class town of Cathcart could provide. When it came time for college, there was no hesitation. Nick had pursued a career in architecture and building design, and he, Charles, had gone off to law school. And he was grateful to the Seymours for believing in him, and for providing him with the home and family life he might otherwise have been denied.

He had signed up with the local firm employed by his uncle — no surprise there. He had settled in and quietly begun to make a name for himself. He was not a splashy lawyer, but steady, and with a knack for research that soon made him indispensable to his colleagues in ferreting out the obscure, precedent-setting case that might apply to a sticky situation at hand. Even these days, when he returned from Phoenix for his frequent check-ins with Connie and Gail and visits with his aunt and uncle, he enjoyed walking the streets of his old stomping grounds, greeting his old Scout-master at the local hardware store, holding the door for a former teacher at the bank, and shaking the hand of the family's church pastor.

But not this time. He had not dared show his face in town, choosing to hole up in his room at the Seymour house, or in this spare office at the law firm. He was afraid of being drawn into a debate by locals who would all be buzzing about the new horror and wanting his opinion on the guilt or innocence of Damon Powell, especially given his proximity to the case on both fronts — as a known partner to the defense team, and his more painful connection to the Seymour family.

And it was even more difficult skirting the issue with his aunt and uncle. He knew exactly how they felt. Both were now convinced that Damon had to be guilty of this new heinous crime, and they could not comprehend just how and why he would choose to help the very people who were trying to keep Damon free. Charles did not know the young man beyond what had come out at the first trial and the few comments that had been made about him in the intervening years by his colleagues. Gail and Connie, and Hugo for that matter, all seemed to believe the young man was innocent.

Charles thought about that for a moment. After all this time, his friends must surely have had enough contact with the young man to make an educated observation about his character. And he, Charles, trusted his friends and colleagues — with his life, if it came to that. In fact, he credited Hugo with saving his life during that frightening episode at Cliffside several years ago. He knew now he was never in any real danger at the time, but it had felt that way to him. And he would never forget the relief he felt when Hugo entered that little fisherman's hut to rescue him.

If he had to stake his life on it, he would trust all three of them to make the very best decisions possible, given the limitations of availability of evidence and knowledge of the accused's character. And it was time now for Charles to make a decision. Not based on fear or loyalty to family, but on plain common sense and regard for his companions' integrity and intelligence. He got up with purpose, returned the un-opened soda to the refrigerator, grabbed his jacket and headed out the door.

'I'm going out for a while,' he said to the receptionist, checking to make sure she had his cell phone number. 'Call me immediately if anyone here needs me, or if anything comes up about one of my cases.' He handed her a list of the cases in question. 'I'll be back in an hour or so.'

He rang for the elevator, went to the ground floor and headed out to retrieve the car Uncle Floyd had loaned him. It was time to fish or cut bait, as the old saying went. And he had no intention of being a bystander.

★　★　★

By the time he returned it was mid-afternoon, and he was afraid everyone would be gone on errands of their own. But when he inquired at the front desk, he was told, 'No, Ms. Brevard and Mr. Osterlitz are still in her office. Shall I ring them?'

'No, that's all right. I'll just look in.' Before the woman could say anything further, he opened the double doors leading to the hallway and walked through. He could hear muffled voices emanating through Gail's door, and hesitated a moment. Then he rapped on the door, and as Gail's voice sang out, 'Come in,' he opened it and walked through.

There was a momentary silence as two pairs of eyes, Gail's and Connie's, looked up questioningly; and a third set, belonging to Damon Powell, looked at him warily.

'Oh, hi, Charles,' Connie said. 'We're just reviewing some things with Damon. Is there anything you need? Problem with one of the cases?'

'No, no,' Charles said a little hastily. 'Look, there's something I need to discuss with you, and there's no easy way to go about it. I hate to take up your time, but I've got to clear the air.'

Damon grabbed the notepad in front of him and moved to rise.

'Wait, Damon,' Charles went on. 'This concerns you, too. I wish Hugo was here, but I can talk to him later.'

'Sit down, Charles,' said Connie, gesturing to the empty chair next to him. 'We're due for a break anyway, I think. Coffee?' he added, almost as an afterthought.

'No, I've had lunch. The thing is …' He paused. This was going to be more difficult than he thought. 'The thing is, I wanted to have an honest discussion with you about my role here, and also about the … Damon's case.' He nodded at the young man sitting quietly across the table from him.

'I think I know where you might be going with this, Charles,' Gail said. She paused and looked down at her notes, as if she might find an answer there. 'If you're having second thoughts about being here, with all this going on, well, I can certainly understand that. I know it must be very difficult for you, given your close connection with the Seymour family.' She glanced at Damon to see how he was taking this.

'No, that's not it at all.' Charles suddenly felt overheated, stood up and took his jacket off, folding it over the back of the chair, and then took his seat again. He looked around the table at each of them. 'I just … I wanted you all to know that I have full confidence in all of you — including you, Damon. I've come to a decision, and I thought it was important that I tell you all immediately, rather than piecemeal. I've just come back from moving out of the Seymour house and into the hotel down the street. I had a long talk with my aunt and uncle, to try and make them understand my dilemma. I can't be a lawyer just part of the time, and as much as I love and care for them, I can't be around them during this crisis. Each time they see me, it brings back their pain again. I can't … I won't do that to them, or to myself either. It's not right, and it's not ethical.'

'You said you've taken a room at the hotel,' Connie began. 'Does that mean you intend to stay until the end of the trial? Would you rather not work on our cases here? We'll be okay with that, if that's your decision. There are several other attorneys in town who'd be glad of the work, I think.'

'That's not what I mean at all, Connie. I intend to stay right here, working on your other cases as needed. But more importantly, I want you to use me in whatever way you think is best, to do everything possible to establish Damon's innocence.'

There was a gasp from Damon, who put his head down in his hands, shoulders

144

heaving. Gail reached over and patted his shoulder.

'And you don't think you'll have a problem with that?' she said quietly, her eyes searching Charles's.

'None at all. I've given this quite a bit of thought since I've been here. I realized that you and Connie — and Hugo too, of course — are the best friends, colleagues and mentors I have in the world. If you all believe in Damon, then I do, too. I don't know him as well as you all do, but I trust your judgment, and I owe you every bit of loyalty and assistance I can muster.' He sat back, drained, but relaxed now, probably for the first time since he had stepped off the plane.

'One more thing,' he said. 'There's something crucial; something we learned from the first incident five years ago. I've been wracking my brains to think of it, and it'll come to me. We're missing something from that first trial. You know me; I'm a stickler for the details. There's something in all the evidence gathered from the first trial that'll give us some help here. I'm convinced of it. Gail, I need to see all the old files from the first case. I think the answer, or at least part of it, is in that paperwork. I'll keep up on the other briefs, but I'm going to spend every spare moment I can sifting through those notes. If there's an answer there, I'll find it.'

The door opened and Hugo came in, a sheaf of papers in his hand. He glanced at Damon, then looked at Connie and shook his head slightly.

Gail stood up. 'Damon, why don't you go with Charles to the vault and see if you can help him find those files he wants to review? I need to walk around a bit; get the kinks out.'

The vault was a storage room in the basement of the building where Osterlitz and Brevard stored their retired briefs, at least those they deemed important enough to keep for a good long time. Gail walked over to the door with Charles and Damon, explaining where the boxes in question might be located, as best she could remember. She also described which notes might be most rewarding.

'Are you okay with this?' she asked Damon. The files in question dealt with his previous defense trial — the one involving the death of Charles's cousin, Vivian Seymour. This would not be an easy task for either of them, especially Damon.

'I'm fine, Gail,' he said. 'I'm just glad to stay busy. Keeps my mind off the arraignment.'

The pretrial hearing to determine if there was enough evidence to try Damon Powell for the murder of Marilyn Watson was scheduled in two days. The team was scrambling to find any scrap of evidence establishing his innocence, or the possibility of a different assailant, before they went to court.

'Good,' Gail said. 'Now go on, you two. See if you can find something useful in those old notes of mine.'

As the two men headed down the hall, she turned back into the room. 'All right, Hugo. I take it you managed to lay hands on the preliminary autopsy reports. I won't ask you how you got them, but let's try and get through them before Damon returns. I don't want him to have to see them just yet. It doesn't serve any purpose, and will only depress him more than he is already, if that's possible.'

Hugo began to spread out the paperwork on the table. 'Take a deep breath, guys. This isn't for the fainthearted.'

15

Lucy Verner sat in the sunroom of the Norris home in Long Hills and stared out at the snow-covered birdbath. One lone bird perched forlornly on the edge of the ornamental sculpture, pecking resolutely at the icy pool at its feet. Lucy felt the same way, she supposed, as the bird. Alone, and somewhat forlorn.

Cousin Alberta was bustling about in the kitchen, putting together Erle's favorite lunch: tomato soup and grilled cheese sandwiches, with a good helping of crunchy potato chips. She had turned down Lucy's offer to help, which was all right. She didn't particularly enjoy cooking, and wasn't very good at it, in any case. But that wasn't the real problem.

Late last night, after Erle had been tucked away in bed, Lucy attempted to draw Alberta into a discussion about Erle's future. But the older woman had shrugged off her questions, and she had had to be tactfully careful to disengage from the conversation without veering off into a quarrel.

'I don't really see what the problem is,' Alberta had said, knitting needles clacking away on one of her endless winter scarf-cap-and-gloves projects. 'Erle's perfectly all right now. He just had a little bout of impish nonsense, that's all.' She pulled at the skein of brightly colored wool peeking out of the work bag at her side. 'I'm aware now that I have to watch him more closely, and I'm perfectly able to do that,' she added. 'He's really just a little boy at heart, and I don't see why you all are so worried about what he might do, or where he might go. He's not capable of doing anything more devilish than a five-year-old might.' She clenched her jaw tight, eyes shining brightly with righteous indignity.

'I understand how you feel, Bertie,' Lucy said, using the familiar nickname from childhood. 'But you have to realize that, even though he has the sensibilities of a five-year-old, he has the body and strength of a grown man. Given his lack of … ' She struggled for the right words. ' … sophistication, it would be very easy for an unscrupulous individual to take advantage of him; even convince him to do something that might not otherwise occur to him.'

'Now, Lucy, who in the world around here would dream of such a thing?' Alberta stopped knitting, crumpled up the unfinished project in a tight ball and thrust it down into the depths of the work basket. 'I'm very tired, after all that's been going on. I need to get to bed so I'll be fresh when Erle gets up in the morning. Good night.' And with that she had marched off to her room next to Erle's.

Lucy had cleared up the mugs of cocoa they had shared, glanced around the kitchen to see if anything needed to be put away, checked the locks and turned out the lights as she made her way across the foyer to the guest area.

This morning, when she rose at her usual early hour, she had found Erle dressed rather untidily and pacing restlessly beside the slider to the yard, looking longingly out towards the street beyond. Alberta was nowhere to be found, presumably still asleep in her bed.

'Good morning, Erle,' she had said, hoping to draw him into one of their little talks about nature and the sorts of birds that might still be about on such a snowy day.

'Not good, Lucy,' he grumped. 'Not a good morning! I'm ... I'm pooky!' 'Pooky' was his made-up word for restless or antsy.

'What are you pooky about, Erle? Would you like me to fix you some breakfast? How about a nice bowl of cereal?'

'No! Don't want no cereal! Don't want nothin'.'

'But you should have something to eat,' she said soothingly. 'That will make your tummy feel better.'

'Don't want my tummy to feel better. No, No, No!'

'All right,' she said, turning away into the room. 'Let me know if you change your mind.' She had learned long ago that it did no good to argue with him when he was in a mood like this. It was best to just wait it out, letting him get over it on his own.

But Erle hadn't gotten over it at all. He had stomped off to his playroom, where he banged doors and slammed toys about for the next hour or so, until Alberta made her way sleepily into the kitchen looking for coffee. Lucy wondered if this was the pattern every day, and if Alberta even realized how long Erle had been waiting for her unsupervised. This was one of the issues concerning her this morning.

But the other issue was even more unsettling. Gail had taken her aside when she first arrived to discuss the concerns she and Connie had. One of the first things she mentioned was Erle's confrontation with the police, followed by his examination at the hospital. When Gail mentioned the scratches the police said they'd found on her brother's back, all sorts of red flags began unfurling in Lucy's mind. Being a nurse, she was not exactly naïve when it came to the possibilities.

'Oh Lord, Gail! What in the world could he have gotten up to?'

'Exactly. I tell you, Lucy, we really need to get a handle on this before anything else happens. I don't even want to think about the ramifications, especially right now with this legal case pending. But I must. I don't think Mother's able to deal with this sort of thing.'

'Have you told her? I understand she must've seen the scratches, but have you talked to her about what it might mean?'

'Not really. She's in a kind of denial right now. I didn't want to upset her any more than necessary. Not until we have a clearer picture of what we're dealing with. Do you think it'd serve any purpose to have him evaluated again? We've done that so many times, but it's been quite a while. He seemed sort of stable, so we hoped he might just go on in the same manner, without this sort of problem.'

'Alberta's not going to like it, Gail. But I believe you're right. I really think he needs to be evaluated again, with the main emphasis on his adult physical capability coupled with his childlike mental capacity. Let me talk to her about it. Maybe I can convince her it's time to take another look at the situation.'

And that was what she had tried to do. But no matter how tactful, how caring, she tried to be, Alberta resented any implication that she was not 'doing her job' in caring for Erle. And it was obvious she was going to fight any such suggestions for changing or altering their current living situation.

The bird finally tired of chipping away at the ice and flew away.

16

The old shack shivered in the wind. This was something new, this strong, gusty gale from the north. Hal Watson shook himself alert. Each creak and snap of a branch outside the cabin caused him to start and look anxiously about. He was getting paranoid now, he sensed. He was still concerned that his abductor had somehow made the trek to his sanctuary and was even now plotting to break in and overwhelm him.

He had been here long enough that he had developed a sort of ironic twist on the Stockholm syndrome, this time with a place not a person. This structure was *his* now, to defend from all encroachers. He identified with it, and almost cherished it, for providing him warmth and shelter from the elements. The comforting cups of hot tea and the cozy fire had become his everything. And the primitive cabin had become more than a home — it was his castle.

The door rattled again. This time more insistently.

Hal got up from his comfy chair, rubbed his aching left shoulder, and took the loaded pistol in hand. Once more, as he had done dozens of times since that first night, he crept stealthily in sock feet to the entrance and weighed whether or not to open the door — to whatever was on the other side. Each time he had done so previously, the only thing discernible was the expanse of porch defined by a crude pine branch railing overlooking a sea of white stretching into the horizon beyond.

This time was different. As he slowly unlatched the lock and pulled the door toward him, a wraith-like creature rose up and flailed inward, visible steam emanating in a silky swirl from flared nostrils. Hal raised the gun to take aim and fire — then stopped himself.

'No!' he gasped. 'It can't be!'

Then Hal Watson stumbled backward, away from the ghostly apparition, holding up his hands in front of him as if to ward off some evil spirit. He fell to the floor, as blessed oblivion overcame him. His last conscious thought was, *Why is this happening?* Then peaceful dreams took over, and he knew nothing more.

17

'Damn him!' Gail shook her fist in the air. 'I should have known Turner would have a hand in this!'

'What do you mean?' Connie leaned over to see what part of the autopsy report she was referring to.

'This!' Her finger shook as she pointed at the page in front of her. 'It's blackmail, pure and simple! And if he thinks I'll go down without a fight, he's got another thing coming!'

'I know,' said Hugo. 'It took me a bit at first to figure out what all that meant. But I think you might be right about that. Looks to me as if they're intending to show it to us at the arraignment, then hope we'll fold without a fight. The bastards. That's hitting below the belt, in my book. Dunno what we can do about it, but there's no way we can let Damon take the fall for this. Trouble is, I don't see any way around the other part of it, without collateral damage ... ' His voice trailed off.

Connie read swiftly through the section in question, then shook his head in disbelief. 'You really think Turner's behind this?'

'Sure do,' Gail said. 'I'm certain he intended to prosecute this as soon as he got wind of it. He's probably on Charlie's speed dial for such things.' She narrowed her eyes. 'He's been riding pretty high as D.A. for the past two terms. And, of course, I don't think he's ever forgiven me for besting him at Damon's earlier trial.'

Gail was referring to Turner Redland, Cathcart's current district attorney. He and Gail had attended law school together and, for a brief time, had had a romantic fling. That relationship had gone down in flames, and there was nothing romantic about their relationship these days. Gail was already dreading facing him down in court again over this new atrocity. But the forensic evidence she and her team had just discovered was alarming, and could be extremely damaging to her if it came out during the trial, as it most certainly would.

'Do we tell Damon about this?' Connie wondered. 'And what about Charles, since he's now on board with the defense?'

'What?' Hugo looked at Connie quizzically. 'What's this about Charles becoming part of the defense team?'

'He's apparently had a change of heart,' Gail said. 'He's decided that his loyalties lie with us, and you, too, Hugo. He wants to be a full-fledged member of the team, starting now. He had a talk with the Seymours about it this afternoon, and has now moved into the hotel for the time being. Even more important, he thinks he recalls something that came out during the first trial that might be a clue. He and Damon are down in the vault right now, going through the old files from the Seymour case.'

'Well, I'll be … ' Hugo scratched the stubble on his chin. He hadn't had a chance to shave for the past twenty-four hours, as he scrambled about town checking his sources and keeping his operatives busy.

Gail had been mulling over the dilemma uncovered in the as-yet unreleased autopsy records. 'Hugo, do you think you or one of your operatives might be able to get a look at some of those hospital records?'

'Sorry, Gail. The people over there know

us all by sight. They run the other way when they see us coming. All we ever get from them is 'patient confidentiality.' '

'But in this case, mightn't we able to … ?'

'I've got an idea,' said Connie. 'And I think it just might get us what we need. Let me make a phone call and see if the person I have in mind would be willing to do a little undercover work for us.' He left the conference table and moved over to Gail's desk, where he buzzed for an outside line.

Just then the door swung open. Charles entered, followed closely by Damon, carrying a large filing box which he placed on the table.

'Hello, Hugo,' Charles said. 'Good to see you. Have they told you what's up?'

'Sure have, Mr. C.' Hugo reached out and offered his hand. 'Glad to have you on board. We could use your brand of common sense, since so much of this case doesn't make any sense at all.'

'Well, hold on to your hats. Damon and I have come across some interesting tidbits buried in all that paperwork left over from the first trial. This item in particular, Gail, I think will capture your interest.'

Gail took the memo pad Charles held out and began to peruse it carefully. 'Hugo, bring them up to date on the new piece of evidence you've uncovered in the preliminary autopsy report. We might not need anything else, if this is true. Of course, that'd open up a whole other can of worms.'

Hugo, after warning Damon about the nature of what he was about to reveal, passed over the page in question. The office fell silent as the two read and digested the new material. Then Gail passed her sheet on to Hugo without comment.

'Well, just as I thought,' Connie said, returning from his phone call at the desk. 'The lady is willing — and extremely able, I might add. I think we can get those medical records without any difficulty, if my little scheme works.'

He nodded at Charles and Damon then looked curiously at the paper Hugo had just reviewed. 'What's this? Something else?'

Gail nodded. 'Charles and Damon have found the odd bits of information he remembered from our first investigation. Leave it to him to home in on the one critical fact we've all been missing up to now.'

Connie grabbed the note and pored over it. 'I think you're right, Gail,' he said finally, handing it back to Hugo, who added it to their growing file of evidence. 'Don't they live near Hal Watson and his daughter?'

'Yes,' Charles said. 'I've already asked the Seymours' handyman to put together all the surveillance videos from their CRTs taken on that night. Problem is, with the size of those estates out there in Long Hills, sometimes there's not a clear sightline from one house to the next. Still, it might show something on the main road. Hal Watson's car leaving the area, for instance. But the thing is, the people in question are close enough, they might actually have gotten something on video — if they have surveillance cams in service, that is.'

'Hugo, could you send a couple of your best people out there to see if they'd allow us to review any video they might have from that night?' Gail said. 'It'd be best to go about it in a casual way, not raise any suspicion as to our real motive. And, of course, we shouldn't mention anything at all about — '

'Yeah, I've got just the pair,' Hugo said.

'An older couple, been with me a long time. They're very good at this sort of thing. I'll explain it to them thoroughly, about what to say and what not to say. At the very least, we might be able to determine when Hal left, or was forced to leave, and what direction he took. Might be a major factor in finding his whereabouts. I'll get right on it.' So saying, he shoved back his chair, retrieved his jacket and headed out the door.

'All right,' said Gail. 'I think we have a plan now. Damon … ' She looked over at him and her eyes misted over. 'I think we might just have a way out of this mess. It's not going to be easy for any of us. But I do believe we're on the right track. At last.'

Damon Powell gulped and looked at each one of them in turn. 'I really thought I was lost. If you can save me, as you seem to think you can, I'll never be able to repay you. I will owe you my life. I want you all to know I understand that.'

'We're all in this together, Damon,' said Gail. 'More than you know. If we can pull this off, you don't need to repay us. Just pay it forward.'

18

The neatly dressed middle-aged couple hesitated at the front veranda before gingerly climbing the several steps to the front door. The long meandering drive into the estate had been cleared of snow, as had the walkway areas, but ice was still a hazard. The man held the woman's elbow firmly until they were safely under the protective portico. He checked the address on a card clipped to the front of the folder he held. Then he rang the bell. The deep-toned 'bong' echoed throughout the lower floors of the house.

After a few moments, the door opened to reveal a fresh-faced young woman whose best features were her sparkling blue eyes. 'Yes? May I help you?' she said.

'Hello,' the man said politely. 'We're the Johnsons. We're here representing the neighborhood watch group for this area. I wonder if the gentleman and lady of the house are in and could give us a few

166

moments of their time?'

Luanne Riley made a quick judgment. She was familiar with the organization mentioned and was a firm supporter. She knew for a fact that her employers had hosted several meetings of the group in the past. These people looked decent and seemed all right.

'Please come in,' she said, holding the door for them as they scuffed their feet on the thick welcoming mat and made their way in to the foyer. 'May I take your coats? You can wait in the den while I see if they're ready to receive visitors.'

'Thank you so much,' Mr. Johnson said, handing off his topcoat to the maid and assisting his wife in removing hers. 'This is very kind of you.'

Luanne settled the Johnsons in the den, and after enquiring if they would take coffee, which they declined, scurried off to the nether parts of the house. Ten minutes later Mr. Riley entered the den, followed closely by his wife. Introductions were made; and once everyone was seated, he fixed Johnson with a steady eye.

'I don't seem to remember meeting you

at previous meetings. You say you're here representing the watch committee, but I'm wondering what this is all about.'

'Yes, of course. My wife and I haven't been residents here very long, but one of the first things we did was join the group. We come from a much more urban area — ' He named an industrial community to the northeast of Cathcart. '— and we've had our share of battles with crime and things like graffiti and vandalism. We wanted to be sure we were part of the neighborhood, and we're committed to looking out for our neighbors, just as we hope they will do for us.'

'I see. Welcome to the neighborhood … and welcome to our group. We can always use dedicated members willing to help make a difference. But what is it we can do for you today?'

'Well,' Johnson began, 'I'm sure you've heard the news about the … the horrible murder that took place a few days ago … and so close by, too.'

'Yes, yes … it's terrible. We know the Watsons, of course. That was right down the road from us. So the neighborhood watch is involved in this?'

'We're hoping to cooperate with the authorities by canvassing all the close-by neighbors to learn if anyone saw or heard anything that night that might be of assistance.'

'We'll do what we can to help,' Mr. Riley replied. 'But to be honest, these places are so far apart, and noise doesn't travel that far. We were out the evening the tragedy occurred and didn't hear about it until the next day. If we'd known what was going on down there, of course, we would've called the authorities immediately. But, sad to say, we were as much in the dark as everyone else seems to be.'

'So you were away from home that evening. What about servants or other family members?'

'We'd given the servants the night off. We were attending a big gala at the country club that night, and there was no need for them to be on duty. Our daughter is away at school, so there was no one here at the time they say this all happened.'

'What about surveillance cameras? Do you have any kind of security system that might have captured movement of any kind?' Johnson's pen paused above his notepad.

'The cameras? You know I didn't think of that. Again, we're pretty far apart from the other houses. Still, you know it's possible the cameras might have caught Hal Watson's car leaving the area. I understand he's missing. I certainly hope he'll be found soon.'

'So do you still have the video tapes from that evening? Do you mean the police haven't questioned you about this very thing?'

'The police haven't questioned us about anything,' Luanne put in. She had remained silent until this point. 'And I don't understand that. You'd think they'd be going through the whole area, asking people about this. I'm glad *somebody's* making the effort,' she said, with a nod toward the Johnsons.

Her husband stood up. 'Come with me, Mr. Johnson. The ladies can wait here where it's comfortable. Let's go scare up those tapes. I don't do anything with them until the first of each month. All the ones from November should still be intact.'

Half an hour later, the Johnsons waved goodbye to their new friends and made their way back down the slippery steps to their modest mid-size car parked in front of the house.

'Well?' asked Mrs. Johnson, as they climbed in and started back down the long driveway to the main street leading through Long Hills.

'Success,' responded Mr. Johnson. 'Hugo's going to be very happy with this one.'

19

'Could you direct me to the charge nurse, please?' Lucy Verner, dressed in her most uniform-like shirtdress, the 30-year pin she had received at the last county nurses function displayed proudly on her chest, paused at the guard's station just inside the ER at Community Hospital.

'Yes'm. May I ask what your business is?' The uniformed guard looked her over from behind the Plexiglass shield that protected him from the general population.

She held up the papers in her hand. 'I have some paperwork I need to turn in for my family members. It's important I get these to the right person.'

The guard hesitated a moment, then decided the neat middle-aged woman in front of him looked harmless enough. 'All right, ma'am. Just go through those double doors to your left there, go down the hall, and it's the second door on the right. Can't miss it. I'll ring ahead and tell them to expect you.

What's your name?'

'Lucy Verner, representing the Norris family. A member was treated here several days ago, and this is just a follow-up.'

'Okay, I'll buzz you on through.' The guard hit a release button and the doors slid open as Lucy approached. She waved at the guard and went on through.

Finding the proper door, Lucy knocked lightly then entered. An older woman in a plain dark suit sat behind a desk covered in neat stacks of files. She looked up questioningly as Lucy approached, then gestured to one of the visitor's chairs. 'How may I help you?' she inquired.

'Hello, my name is Lucy Verner, Ms … Wooten?' Lucy read from the identification placard on the front of the desk.

'Yes, go on.'

'I'm from Grand View up north. I've retired recently from Olympic General there, and recently I've come to Cathcart to help my cousin, Alberta Norris, with her son, Erle.'

'Oh, the Norris family. Yes, they've been in the area a number of years. How may I assist you?'

'I don't know if you're aware, but Erle Norris was brought to this facility for examination and possible treatment earlier in the week. My query is about him.'

'Yes, I'm familiar with the case. I was on duty the day he was brought in. I didn't actually see or treat him myself, but I discussed the situation with the doctor who was on call that afternoon. Late afternoon, as I recall. I don't believe there was much of anything wrong with him. I think we just checked him over and released him to go home.'

'Yes, that's my understanding also. I didn't come down until a day or two later, but I was told about the incident. You see, my cousin's son is ... I prefer to call him developmentally challenged, for want of a better phrase.'

Nurse Wooten smiled. 'I think that's a good phrase. I much prefer that over other descriptions myself. Do go on. I hope he hasn't had any problems following his visit here.'

'Oh, no,' Lucy said. 'He's doing fine. But just to be on the safe side, his mother's

174

made an appointment to take him to her general practitioner. We were hoping we could obtain records from you of his visit here, just to update his files with his own doctor.'

'I don't think there's much of a record. You are aware, of course, of the patient confidentiality rules? If Mrs. Norris had come in herself ... '

'Oh yes, that's the other thing I wanted to do. I have here ... ' She dug into the tote at her feet. 'Here they are. I have medical powers of attorney for both Alberta Norris and her son Erle Norris, duly signed and notarized. Also I have my nurse's identification, if that'd be helpful. The family believes it'd be good idea — just as a precaution, of course — for my credentials to be on file here, just in case.'

Nurse Wooten took the papers and perused them carefully. 'Everything seems to be in perfect order here, Ms. Verner. If you'll excuse me for a moment, I'll go make copies of these for our files. I'll also bring back the paperwork from Erle's visit the other day for the family doctor. I don't really think there's much of anything in it, but we'll be happy to comply with your request.'

With that, she scooped up the documents and left the room. While Lucy waited, she went over in her mind the next step. It would need to be letter-perfect.

When the charge nurse reappeared, she handed Lucy's documents back to her, then produced a thin folder with only two sheets of paper inside. 'This is all we have from Erle Norris's brief visit,' she said. 'I don't know what help it will be, but I agree it's appropriate for his doctor to have these.'

Lucy took the two sheets of paper from the folder and went over them carefully. She shook her head, puzzled. 'According to this, Erle was brought in by two off-duty officers who said they found him wandering in a field several miles from his home. The doctor ordered his vitals to be taken — blood pressure, temperature, etcetera; had his extremities checked for frostbite; found nothing significantly wrong with him; and released him to return home. Is this all that was done?'

'Why, yes. We took off his shoes and socks to check his toes; checked his fingers, of course, and the tips of his ears and nose. He showed no sign of trauma or damage from the elements, even though he was only dressed in street clothes. He must not have been out very long. Why do you ask?'

Lucy paused. Everything hung on the next few moments. 'But what about the scratches on his back? I see no record of that here at all.'

'Scratches? What scratches? Ms. Verner, we removed his outer clothing and examined him thoroughly. He was cold and shivering, so we wrapped him in a blanket. As for scratches … ' She shook her head. 'I have no idea what you're talking about. There were no such abrasions on his body at all. Are you suggesting he was somehow injured while he was here?'

'Oh no, I'm not suggesting anything of the sort,' Lucy said. 'But the officers who picked him up claimed they noticed scratches on him, and I verified that later at home myself. By the way,' she added almost casually, 'what happened to those officers? Did they stay while Erle was examined, or … where did they go afterwards?'

'Hmmm. You know, that's a little odd.

Yes, they did stay while we checked him out; and while we were trying to get hold of his family, they asked if they could speak with him for a few minutes. We allowed them to use a private room that was empty at the time. They couldn't have been in there more than half an hour when your family members showed up. My recollection is the officers spoke to them a bit as well, before they left.'

'Are you familiar with these officers? Did they leave their names?'

'I think their names are right there in the folder, as the people who brought the young man in. My understanding was that they were off-duty policemen, but if so, I'm not familiar with them. Is anything wrong, Ms. Verner?'

Lucy glanced through the folder once more and confirmed that the two officer's names were indeed recorded there. She assured Nurse Wooten that everything was fine, thanked her profusely for her time and assistance, and made her way back out through the ER to the parking lot.

She had done her very best, she reflected, as she climbed back into her car and headed back towards the Norris house. But this new information was puzzling and seemed sinister to her.

Now it was up to Connie and Gail to make sense of this mystery.

20

'Let's go over everything one more time,' Gail said. 'There must be something we're missing here.'

Damon shook his head to clear the cobwebs, stood up and stretched, then walked over to the window to gaze out once more at the somber sky. Even the weather seemed to echo his miserable thoughts.

'I'm all tapped out, Gail,' he said. 'I've been over everything so many times now, I feel like I could recite it all forwards and backwards.'

'I know, Damon,' she said, getting up to join him at the window. 'But you know as well as anyone that there's always something new, some little detail no one else has thought of. Please, just humor me. I *know* there must be something else we're missing.'

Damon rejoined the group at the table. He felt like he'd been sitting there so long he must have left a permanent dent in the chair. Resolutely, he picked up where he had left off. 'That day was like any other in our lives. I can't remember anything different at all. We both had classes, Mari and I, but we went in separately because our schedules were slightly different. The one thing I remember most of all is planning to have an early dinner together, just to catch up on things. We tried to do that as often as possible, just because we were both so busy — ' His voice cracked, and he looked away quickly to hide his tears.

Hugo spoke up. 'You say you went in separately to school? I know you drove your car, but how about Marilyn? Did she drive her own car, or take public transportation? I seem to recall you saying she went back to Hal's office at some point?'

'Yes, she did,' Damon said, looking up. 'But she didn't drive herself; she carpooled. There was another student whose schedule was similar. They agreed at the beginning of the term to take turns driving in. I believe that person must have dropped her off at Hal's office after their last class.'

'And then she went home with her father?'

'Yes. I'd arranged to pick her up at their house when I got out of class. Then we went to dinner, just as I said before.'

'Did she mention this person's name, the person she was carpooling with? Male or female?'

'It was another woman, about Marilyn's age I think. She was from out of town, so I didn't know her. I know she mentioned her name. Hal would know — ' He broke off abruptly.

'Think, Damon,' Connie broke in. 'This might be very important. You said she mentioned she had the feeling someone might've been following her. Do you think it could be this person?'

'No, I don't think so. I got the impression it was someone she didn't know, something like that.'

Hugo had been glancing at his phone and got up abruptly. 'Excuse me a minute. I've got people reviewing the CRT tapes we've gotten from several different sources. They're telling me they might have an important lead.' He left the room.

'Did you ever see this other driver?' Gail asked. 'Do you know what she looked like?'

'Not that I recall,' Damon said. 'But I know at one time she kind of laughed about it, and called the other woman her birthday twin. Seems they were born just a day apart, so they'd made a little joke about it. Damn, why didn't I think of all this before?'

'It's all right,' Gail said. 'It probably doesn't mean a thing to our investigation. But I'm glad you remembered it, all the same. If we can find the woman, she might be able to add another piece to the puzzle. Maybe she noticed this person following Gail as well.'

The intercom buzzed and Hugo's voice came over. 'Get down to my office,' he said. 'All of you, now. I think we might have uncovered something that'll help.'

Silently, the four at the table — Connie and Gail, Damon and Charles — rose and hurried out of the office and down to Hugo's domain.

What had Hugo's people discovered? And would it help or hurt their case?

21

The court room slowly filled up. This was only the arraignment, a hearing to determine if there was enough evidence to bring Damon Powell to trial for the murder of Marilyn Watson. But feelings were running high in the case. The citizens of Cathcart were horrified at what had transpired in their midst; in the very best part of town, no less. If the murdered woman had been a prostitute from the wrong side of the tracks, not nearly as much interest would have been generated. But she had been one of their own. Not only that, but it also appeared to be the handiwork of the same villain who had killed Vivian Seymour some five years earlier. Many believed that Damon Powell had been involved in the first incident, and had, through trickery and connivance, gotten off scot-free.

Now the same murderer had struck again, or so it seemed. This time the killer must be forced to pay for his crimes. If

Damon wasn't guilty, as his defenders claimed, then who was? No one in their right mind wanted someone running around loose who might strike again, at any time, and wreak havoc at will.

So the citizens filled up the seats quickly, following in behind the main players and, of course, the press, who took up a full row just by themselves. A sketch artist had been brought in as well, since TV cameras were not allowed.

The room buzzed with excitement *Just like a hive of angry bees*, thought Gail as she took her seat at the defense table, Connie beside her, and Charles and Hugo seated in the row immediately behind. She glanced over at the prosecutor's area. Yes, just as she thought — there was Turner, smiling broadly at his supporters surrounding him. Behind the table, one whole row was taken up with Charlie Hudson and his crew. They all seemed very sure of themselves, she thought, and she pondered the revelations the day's questioning would bring, and how they all would react.

'All rise,' the bailiff called out, and there was the usual scraping of feet and rustling of clothing as the entire court room rose to greet Judge Harriman as he entered and took his place at the head of the bench. Once all were seated again, and the judge had looked over the file placed in front of him, he took a sip of water, cleared his throat and began.

'Damon Powell, you are charged with the crime of murder in the first degree. How do you plead?'

Damon responded in a steady voice, 'Not guilty, your honor.'

'Do you have representation?'

Gail stood. 'Yes, your honor. The firm of Osterwitz and Brevard are acting as defense for the defendant.'

Harriman looked down again and was silent for a moment before directing his attention to the prosecutor's table. 'Is the prosecution prepared?'

'Yes, your honor,' Turner Redland's voice rang out. 'Turner Redland for the people.'

'Opening statements, then. Ms. Brevard, are you ready to proceed?'

'Sidebar, if you please, your honor.' Gail felt a little quiver of excitement run through her as she contemplated her next words.

'So soon?' Harriman sighed. 'Oh well, then. Come forward.' He gestured to Redland as well, and the D.A., his assistant, Connie and Gail all moved to the bench.

'What's this about, Ms. Brevard? Surely we could at least get started before you start throwing up problems.'

'Your honor, the defense would like to move for an immediate dismissal and declaration of a mistrial.'

'On what basis?' Turner was nearly shouting in anger. 'What is your basis for a mistrial?'

'Your honor, if you'll give me a chance — '

'Cease!' Judge Harriman stood and gathered his robes. 'My chambers, all of you, now!'

They followed him back to his private chambers and entered the room behind him. He flung off his robe, took a seat behind his desk, and glared at Gail. 'All right, now. Ball's in your court, Ms. Brevard. What in blazes is this all about?'

Turner spoke up quickly. 'I'd like to put in an objection here, your honor. We've received no prior notification from the defense concerning anything that might be relevant to a mistrial.'

'We've only just discovered this situation during the last twenty-four hours, your honor. We had to be sure of our findings, and we've only just this morning confirmed an alarming lapse on the part of the prosecution in the handling of crucial evidence in this case.'

'Mr. Redland,' intoned the judge, 'please be seated, and let's hear the lady out.'

Turner sat back down, a scowl on his handsome face. He exchanged a questioning look with his ADA, who shrugged her shoulders.

'Thank you,' Gail said. She stood and faced the others in the room. 'This is somewhat complicated, so if you'll just allow me to tell the story from the beginning without interruption, I think our reservations about this case will all come clear.'

'Go ahead, Ms. Brevard,' Judge Harriman said. 'We're all ears.'

'Very well. I need to start with an incident that took place the same afternoon Mr. Powell was arrested. Just after I met with him and the arresting officer for his preliminary questioning, I received an unsettling personal message.'

Turner Redland started to object, but a glare from the judge quieted him.

Gail hesitated. The next few minutes would be crucial. 'I was informed that my brother, Erle Norris, had been picked up and detained by two off-duty officers and taken to Community Hospital for observation.'

'I'm afraid I'm going to have to agree with Mr. Redland here, Counselor,' Judge Harriman interrupted. 'I don't see how this tale has any bearing at all on Mr. Powell's case.'

'Oh but it does, your honor, and I have every bit of proof I need to back it up, if you'll just allow me to continue.'

'Go ahead. But you must make a connection shortly, or I'm afraid I'll have to move this back into the courtroom.'

'Yes. You may or may not know that my brother has special needs. He's an adult chronologically, but he's never advanced beyond the level of a very young child mentally and emotionally. It would not be an exaggeration to say he's gullible and easily manipulated.'

'Yes, but what does this have to do with

Mr. Powell's case?'

'I'm trying to put this as succinctly as possible, your honor, but I assure you this information is all crucial to this trial.' Gail reached into her briefcase and pulled out a small file folder. 'This is the medical record released by the hospital to my family just yesterday. It confirms my brother was checked by a doctor for frostbite, his vitals were taken, and then he was released to the custody of my family.'

'And … ?'

'This is the important part. The off-duty officers who picked him up knew him on sight, and they also knew he was my brother. They spoke to my colleague, Hugo Goldthwaite, at the hospital, saying they were concerned about 'suspicious' scratches my brother had on his back. As you might imagine, this was very upsetting to us.'

'Go on,' Harriman said. This was getting interesting.

'The nurse who was in charge on the day my brother was examined has stated, without equivocation, that *there were no scratches* on Erle's body whatsoever when he was treated. She also stated that at some point the off-duty officers asked to speak to him privately, before he was released to us, and a room was provided for them to do that. When Erle was returned to us later, he *did* have scratches on his back. And I saw them.'

'I don't see what any of this has to do with this case,' Turner said. 'I repeat my previous objection. I think this is all just a waste of time, and defense is trying to throw up some sort of smoke screen.'

'Ms. Brevard?' Judge Harriman looked at her sternly. 'What say you about Mr. Redland's objection?'

'I haven't gotten to the most important aspect of this whole scenario,' Gail said. 'There's a preliminary report from the coroner's office concerning the autopsy of Marilyn Watson. I'm certain the prosecution has had access to it by now, but we were not given a copy.'

Turner started to object again, but Gail cut him off. 'However, through various sources, we *were* able to see a copy of that report, which I'm certain was going to be produced at some point today in order to blackmail my firm into agreeing to some sort of plea bargain for Mr. Powell.'

'That's absurd!' cried Turner Redland, jumping to his feet. 'Are you crazy? What in the world are you talking about?'

Gail stood quietly, watching him with emotions that varied from distaste to amusement at his consternation. 'Your honor,' she said, handing him a document from her folder, 'here's one page of the preliminary autopsy report, which purports to match scrapings from the fingernails of the deceased with the DNA of my brother, Erle Norris. The problem is, your honor, we know Marilyn Watson confronted her slayer on the night *previous* to the afternoon my brother was examined by the hospital. At that time — and the charge nurse on duty at the time will testify to this — he had no scratches on his body at all. Later, when he was returned home, after the off-duty officers had interviewed him privately, there were scratches on his back, and they appeared to be fresh.'

There was total silence in the judge's chambers. Gail stared at Turner Redland. His normally robust complexion had gone ashen. There was a look of disbelief on his face, and he sat quietly. This had not gone how he had expected.

'And so, your honor,' Gail resumed, 'on the basis of our proof that the authorities have tampered with the evidence, I would like at this point to ask for a dismissal of this trial and a complete exoneration of my client.'

'Return to the courtroom,' Harriman said. He, too, looked stunned. 'Ms. Brevard, I'll keep this sheet, if you don't mind. I'll inform you of my decision shortly.' And with that, they all tromped out, leaving Judge Harriman staring off into space. None of them envied him.

As soon as the attorneys re-entered the court room, Turner Redland marched to the row behind his table and loudly called Detective Charlie Hudson forward to the prosecutor's table. Hudson, puzzled, complied, and the two sat huddled in conversation. Redland's face was vivid with anger, and Charlie's arms waved towards two uniformed men seated near the end of the first row. One blurted out something and started to rise, thought better of it, and sat back down. The other officer said and did nothing.

Charlie Hudson rose, approached the bailiff and whispered a few words, gesticulating at a piece of paper in his hand. The bailiff immediately called over two burly guards and gave them instructions. Without any argument, the two unidentified officers were taken into custody and marched away to a holding cell. Hudson returned to his seat, and Turner Redland, red-faced and seething, slammed his briefcase shut and waited for the judge's return.

Gail patted Damon's hand and smiled. 'It's nearly over,' she said.

The bailiff announced Judge Harriman's return. Once again, the court rose in unison and took their seats again. 'Occasionally,' Harriman began, 'an anomaly takes place within the context of a hearing which must be dealt with legally, but may not, on examination, have anything to do with the crime in question.'

'Uh oh,' Gail whispered to Connie. 'I don't like where this is going.'

'We have such a situation before us today. It is my understanding that pre-trial evidence has been tampered with by a party or parties unknown. I've deliberated over the issue and have come to the decision that, as serious as the tampering is, it does not materially alter the facts of the case before us. A heinous crime has occurred in our community. An individual has been apprehended and questioned in regard to that crime. I believe the tampering of evidence is a side issue and has no bearing on the guilt or innocence of the party charged. Therefore my ruling is that the arraignment is still in session. Any further evidence as to the likelihood of the accused's innocence or guilt should be presented by his defense at this time.'

'Your honor,' Conrad Osterlitz said as he stood in response, 'the defense wishes to register an objection to this ruling in anticipation of an appeal.'

'So granted, Mr. Osterlitz. Do you have any further evidence to present as to why your client should not stand trial?'

'Yes, we do.' Connie paused for effect. 'The defense calls ... Oliver Kincaid.'

The audience immediately buzzed with anticipation. The Kincaids were leading lights in the Cathcart community. Mr.

Kincaid was currently in charge of the chamber of commerce, and Mrs. Kincaid was president of the women's club.

'And,' Connie added as the well-dressed, gray-haired gentleman was escorted from the holding area to be sworn in, 'we wish permission to treat Mr. Kincaid as a hostile witness.'

'Granted,' said Harriman.

Once Kincaid was sworn in and recited his name for the record, Connie proceeded. 'Mr. Kincaid, you and your wife currently reside in the Long Hills area.' He stated this as a fact, not a question.

'Yes.'

'How long have you lived at your present address?'

'We've been on the same property for approximately 25 years.'

'Can you give an approximation of the distance from your front entrance, say, to the home of Harold and Marilyn Watson?'

'As the crow flies? Very close, about 100 yards at most. It's a little longer than that, if you go down our drive, down the main street and back up their driveway. But a straight shot, from our house to theirs? About the length of a football field would be my guess.'

'At present, you and your wife reside in your house, along with several servants?'

'Yes.'

'And you also have a daughter?'

'Laura, yes. But she's away at school right now. Fall term.'

'Just the one daughter, yes. And what school is she attending? How far is it from Cathcart?'

Oliver Kincaid hesitated and looked at the judge. 'Do I need to answer these questions, your honor? I hate to have my daughter's information put out all over.'

Connie spoke up. 'Your honor, please direct the witness to answer the questions. I will connect my line of questioning with the case at hand.'

'Very well, Mr. Osterlitz, you may continue. But I'm warning you — you must connect all this quickly. Please answer the question.' Harriman directed the last toward Kincaid.

'Laura is attending the Culinary Institute in Brockhurst,' he said finally. 'It's about a day's drive from here.'

'Does she return home from time to time? Weekends, holidays and the like?'

'From time to time. Not if she's studying or has some function to attend at school, but yes, from time to time she comes home for the weekend.'

'When was the last time she came home?'

Kincaid paused. He appeared to be thinking back to when such an event occurred, but he could also be giving himself time to come up with a suitable answer. 'I believe she was last at home two weeks ago. But I'd have to ask my wife to be sure.'

'We might do that, if necessary.' Connie turned back to the table and reached for some papers. 'Do you recall a point in time some five years ago when Ms. Brevard came to your house, at your wife's insistence, and spoke with your daughter?'

'Uh … I'm not sure what you mean.'

Turner was on his feet. 'Objection, your honor. This has got to be the wildest fishing expedition we've ever witnessed. What on earth does any of this have to do with the present case?'

'I'm asking myself the same question, Mr. Redland. Mr. Osterlitz, does this have anything at all to do with your client's defense?'

'I'm trying to get there, your honor. With the court's indulgence, I will make a connection.'

'Very well. But make that connection, and make it quickly.'

Connie turned back to Oliver Kincaid. 'Do you recall the conversation during which your daughter made it clear to Ms. Brevard, in no uncertain terms, that she was sharing an intimate moment with Damon Powell on the very night Vivian Seymour was murdered?'

The gasp rippled through the court room. The judge gaveled for quiet and waited until it was still once more.

Turner Redland scrambled to his feet. 'Objection! Objection! This information has nothing whatsoever to do with our present case!'

Connie spoke quietly, but with authority. 'On the contrary, your honor. We believe this has *everything* to do with the present case. And what's more, we intend to prove it.'

'Silence!' shouted Judge Harriman, as the court burst into an uproar. 'I'm taking a short recess. Everyone back in half an hour, and be prepared to maintain absolute decorum on your return!'

As the court emptied, Gail and Connie gathered their crew together. 'I think we've established doubt,' she said uncertainly. 'But as to a dismissal? I don't know if we can accomplish that or not.'

'We'll do our best,' Connie said. 'That's all we can do. Then let the chips fall where they may.'

22

Hugo had been looking at his phone, a habit Gail often chided him for. 'What's up?' she asked as their group headed off to a conference room for the short duration of the recess.

'I've got to go,' he said, shrugging into his jacket and breaking into a run. 'Try to stall the hearing as long as possible. I may have something — something important ...' His voice faded as he disappeared down the stairs, two at a time, to the ground floor rotunda.

'What the ... ?' Charles looked after his pal, wishing he had been asked to join in. He was feeling antsy, especially after the last bit about Laura Kincaid. That had been the bit of information that had been driving him crazy, until he found the interview with her in Gail's files. If she was so heavily involved in Vivian's murder, what might she know about this new atrocity? Especially since her family home was so close to the

Watson residence.

'All in good time, I guess,' Gail muttered. 'But I do wish Hugo would be more forth-coming about these escapades of his. I hope he gets back before the hearing resumes. We might need him more here than off chasing rumors.'

'Let's try and focus on the situation at hand,' Connie said, drawing them into a private room set aside for attorneys and their clients. 'We need to think where we're going to go next with this. Damon, what's your take on this? *Were* you that heavily involved with Laura Kincaid — at the time of Vivian's death, I mean?'

'Not really.' Damon had been quiet, thinking about all that had gone before, and what it meant for his future now. 'I can't get it out of my mind, though, that I really think she drugged me that night. Why, I don't know, but I think it's a very good possibility. The way I fell so sound asleep … and Dad's gun gone missing. It almost seems like some contrived plot.'

'That's what I'm thinking,' Gail said. 'Is it so far-fetched to think that Laura, as young as she was at the time, could've been responsible for Vivian's death?'

'I don't know. It was terrible, the way she was shot. Butchered, really.'

They all fell silent for a moment, thinking.

'We should move for a continuance of the arraignment,' Gail said. 'In the meantime, we need to subpoena Laura and question her again, this time about her whereabouts on the night Marilyn was killed. It might be enough to cast doubt on the identity of the killer. Laura might have been an accomplice ... but what could be her motivation?'

'I can tell you that,' said Damon. 'Laura Kincaid was extremely jealous of Vivian, and any of the women in her crowd. Anyone who had a social life, was popular with the boys, dated a lot. She was always going on about how unfair life was. She seemed to believe everyone had it in for her, when it wasn't true at all. She had the same advantages as all the other women. She just didn't believe it.'

'I suppose that could be motivation of a sort,' Connie said. 'We'll have to throw it out there, see if it sticks. But I think a continuance will be our best move. We need more time to interview our witnesses, including Laura.'

A discreet knock on the door informed them court was going back in session. As they filed out into the hallway, Gail tried to concentrate on what she would say and do next. Yes, Connie was right. A continuance would be their best bet.

One more time court was called into session, and the bailiff intoned 'All rise' as Judge Harriman entered and took his place at the bench. When all were seated, he looked toward the defense table. 'Any more witnesses, Counselor?'

Gail was just about to reply when the outer door opened and one of Hugo's operatives hurried in and down the aisle. 'One moment, your honor, while I confer with my colleague,' she said, turning to hear what the man had to say. She and Connie listened, speechless, as an animated Abe Johnson relayed Hugo's news.

'Your honor, it appears we *do* have another witness on the way here. If you would give us a brief break to — '

Just as Turner Redland rose to object to

any further delays, the outer door opened again and Hugo gave them a vigorous thumbs-up.

'It's all right, your honor,' Gail said. 'We are prepared to call our next, and final, witness.'

'Very well, Counselor. You may proceed.'

'Thank you. The defense wishes at this time to call ...' She paused for effect. 'The defense wishes to call its final witness, Marilyn Leeann Watson.'

Pandemonium broke out. The judge gaveled in vain for silence, and the bailiff could be heard shouting for order above the noise of the crowd. All heads swiveled to the back of the room.

Damon half-rose in his chair, a variety of emotions flickering across his face. He looked from Gail to Connie in amazement. 'What the ...?'

'Easy, Damon,' Gail said. 'All will be explained in time.' Her eyes misted over as she stood and watched Hugo and Abe's wife, Mildred Johnson, carefully walk an unsteady Marilyn Watson down the aisle to the defense table. Damon was sobbing by now, and it was all Gail could do to keep him from dashing forward and folding Marilyn in his arms. Turner Redland's table had erupted in consternation, and he turned once more to fix Detective Charles Hudson with a riveting stare.

Finally, the young woman, with assistance, moved forward to the witness stand, where she was sworn in and asked her name.

'Marilyn Leeann Watson,' she said in a firm though low-pitched voice.

Even Judge Harriman seemed amazed at the sight. 'Are you able to give testimony, Miss Watson?' he asked. 'Do you need anything? Water?'

'No, I'm all right.'

'Will the defense team proceed, then? But the witness is obviously under strain. I would suggest you not overtax her.'

'Thank you, your honor. We agree,' said Connie with a nod at Gail, who rose to examine her witness, trembling inside but determined.

'Miss Watson, we are so glad you're here,' she began, choking up, then pulling herself together to continue. 'We're so very glad you are here to tell us something of what has occurred to you over the past several days. I'd like to begin with a brief recap of November 3rd, the day in question.'

'Thank you, Ms. Brevard. I'm very thankful to be here as well. I'm prepared to answer any questions you may have.'

'Mr. Powell has told us something of the last evening you spent together. I'd like you now to confirm, in your own words, your own recollection of that time.'

'Yes. We both had classes that day, but at different hours. I chose to carpool with a young woman ... ' She paused and reached out a hand to steady herself, '... who I only knew slightly since the beginning of the term. Our class schedules were similar, and we were coming from the same part of town, so it was very convenient for both of us to take turns driving in to school.'

'I see. Go on.'

'On that particular day she dropped me off at my father's office, and I drove home with him. Damon — Mr. Powell — had planned to pick me up for an early dinner date. We went to the Napoli, a favorite of ours, ate a light meal, talked about the day's events, and he took me back home. All of this in the early evening.'

'Had anything unusual transpired during the day — at school, during your travels back and forth, or later, while you and Mr. Powell were at dinner?'

'In retrospect, I realize that one of my earlier hunches was true. I'd had the feeling, since the beginning of the school term, that someone was stalking me. I didn't have enough information to actually accuse anyone, but Rebecca, the girl I was carpooling with, mentioned she'd felt the same sensation. We talked about it on the way to Dad's office, and the last thing ... the last thing she said to me when I got out of the car was, 'Be careful, Marilyn. I think this might be serious.' '

'Did you mention this to Mr. Powell at dinner?'

'Yes, in passing. I'm afraid I made light of it, and told him it was nothing to worry about.'

'Was there anything unusual about your return home later that evening?'

'Yes. When Damon and I returned to the house, I was surprised to find the front door unlatched. Damon offered to come in and have a look around, but I thought my father had stepped out on the porch for some fresh air then forgot to lock the door behind him when he went back in.'

'So you said good night to Mr. Powell and he left?'

'Yes; we said our goodbyes, and I waved to him before entering the house.'

'And what happened when you went inside?'

There was a brief silence. Marilyn Watson appeared to be lost in thought for a moment.

'Do you need some time, Miss Watson?' the judge said.

'No. Sorry. I was just trying … to put it all in order.'

'Take your time,' Gail urged. 'We can wait.'

'I went inside, and the first thing I noticed was that the foyer light seemed to be out. Dad usually left it on when I was out so I wouldn't have to fumble around in a dark room. While I was reaching for the switch, someone grabbed me from behind and put a cloth over my face. It must've had something like chloroform on it, because I went out like a light. I didn't know anything at all for some time, I guess. When I woke up, I was on the couch in the living room.'

'Was your father there? Were you able to see the person who drugged you?'

'No, Dad wasn't there. I didn't know it then, of course, but what I found out later was that he'd been subdued before I got home. He was locked in the den so he couldn't interfere with ... with what took place later.'

'And what took place, Miss Watson? We know *something* happened in the living room of your home that night, but it obviously isn't what we were led to believe.'

'This is very difficult for me.' Marilyn Watson bowed her head and tears streamed down her cheeks. 'I feel responsible in a way, though I don't know what I could have done differently to prevent this atrocity. You see, the person who died that night *should* have been me; was *supposed* to be me, I'm sure. But it was all just a huge bunch of mistakes.'

'If you weren't the victim, as the police asserted, Miss Watson, then who in God's name was it? Who was killed that night in your home? And why did the police assume it was you?'

'The person responsible definitely had me in mind as the victim, and I believe it was solely because of my relationship with Mr. Powell. You see, this person, long ago, had warned me away from Damon. I'd forgotten that in recent years. But as Damon and I got close and began to plan our marriage, word got out among our friends and acquaintances. It was only a matter of time before this person would learn of it as well. I believe at some point the decision was made to do away with me, in much the same way Vivian Seymour was killed years ago. And, I might add, for the same reason. Pure jealousy.

'The huge mistake that was made that evening, however, was a case of mistaken identity, pure and simple. When the killer decided to do away with me, the first person who came through the door that evening was not me. It was Janet Clemson, my car-pooling buddy. You see, I'd left one of my textbooks in her car that afternoon. She thought I might need it for studying, and decided to drop it by the house. When she got there she found the door ajar, just as I did later. When she stepped inside the darkened foyer, she was ambushed too. The only difference was … she was savagely killed.

'By the time I got there, the killer was so psyched out, the decision was made to make an escape, hoping the police would be as fooled by Miss Clemson's appearance as the killer was. A shot to the face made identification difficult. Our hair colors and styles were similar, and we had the same general body build. To make identification even more difficult, my father was removed from the scene so that he wouldn't be available to the authorities.'

'But why weren't you killed as well?'

'I'm not sure. I think the trauma of that huge mistake was so jarring that the killer began making poor decisions. By the time the stage had been set, I'd been stuffed into the trunk of my father's car. After what felt like hours of a long bumpy ride, I felt the car leave the road and tumble over a precipice. I waited for sounds, or for someone to release me, but there was nothing but silence.'

'Good heavens! How in the world did

you manage to escape?'

'Fortunately I read an article not too long ago about how, since 2002, all cars are manufactured with an interior trunk release lever. It's an easy matter, once you know about it, to pull the lever and release the trunk hatch. When I looked in the back seat of the car I saw my assailant, who appeared to be lifeless. From there I had to climb out of the gulch, in the snow, and try to find shelter.'

'Because you're here, I'm assuming you did manage to find shelter, and from there you were rescued. You're a very lucky young lady.'

'I'm doubly lucky.' And for the first time, Marilyn Watson smiled. 'I might've missed it, if it hadn't been for the chimney smoke. I did find shelter; and when I made my way there, and banged on the door, I got a wonderful surprise.'

At that moment, the doors at the rear opened. All heads turned that direction in curiosity. In a wheelchair, but sitting up and smiling broadly, Hal Watson made an entrance.

'As you can see,' Marilyn said, beaming,

'my wonderful surprise was my father, alive and well. He'd managed to climb out of the abyss, the same as me, and he found the little cabin and took shelter there. The poor man thought I was dead, but he was determined to stay alive to testify as to what happened.'

'And we're all grateful for that,' said Gail. 'By the way, as a matter of curiosity, how did you and your father manage to get back to town? Surely you were both very weak, and with the snow...'

'Well, first I made sure my father was all right. He fainted when I made my unexpected appearance, but soon came around. We talked and decided on an immediate plan of action. You see, I was already afraid that Damon would be the obvious suspect, because of the earlier murder. Both Dad and I were determined to get back and tell our story in order to save him from...' Her voice trailed off.

'And so you set out on foot? With all that snow, and the cold?'

'We bundled up as best we could and set out. It was very difficult, but once we got out to the main fire road, we discovered that the walking wasn't as bad in the light of day as we'd anticipated.'

'But you must've been miles from town.'

'Well, that's just it. We hadn't walked more than a mile or two when here came this four-wheel drive vehicle, lumbering up the road towards us. We flagged it down to discover Mr. Goldthwaite's operatives on their way to save us.'

'But how did they know where to look for you?'

'Apparently they'd reviewed some video surveillance tapes they'd gotten just hours earlier. The tape of the day in question revealed my father's car leaving our driveway shortly after the assault. As they watched, the car headed out away from town on Highway 89, which as you know, turns into the fire road leading into the National Forest. Without that tape, we might be walking on that road still.'

Gail paused to let the court settle down again before resuming. 'My last question, Miss Watson, is crucial to this case. Do you know the identity of the person who assaulted you and your father that terrible evening and took the life of your friend?'

'Yes. And I'm so very sorry to say it, but it was Laura Kincaid. I know it's hard to believe such a beautiful young woman could be capable of committing such a terrible crime, but there is no doubt in my mind about it at all.'

'Thank you, Miss Watson. The defense rests,' said Gail, looking toward the prosecution table. Turner Redland just shook his head. There would be no cross-examination.

'Very well. Case dismissed,' said Judge Harriman, leveling his gavel. 'I order the authorities to make an immediate search for the crashed vehicle in question and retrieve and identify the body inside. I'll make a final ruling on this case once that task has been accomplished. Given the revelations of today, I am ordering that the families of both Laura Kincaid and the young woman who appears to be the real victim in this case be sought out, duly notified, and asked to make proper identification and disposition of the remains. The court and all present, I am sure, offer sympathy for their mutual losses. I am just sorry this whole affair couldn't somehow have been prevented. I also am ordering the district attorney to file charges against the two officers who so callously manipulated vital evidence at the coroner's office, and anyone else who might have been involved in such shenanigans.' He glared at Detective Charles Hudson, before directing his gaze to Damon Powell. 'In the meantime, young man, you are free to go. You are very fortunate to have such staunch friends. This whole thing could have ended very differently. My sincere thanks go out to the firm of Osterlitz and Brevard and their staff, for their professionalism and perseverance. We could use more like you.'

As Gail was gathering her files back into her briefcase, Turner Redland came over. 'Congratulations, Counselor,' he said. 'I hope there are no bad feelings here. I assure you I had nothing to do with that debacle at the coroner's office. We'll be dealing with those scoundrels in due course. I have a feeling Charlie Hudson is in for a very rude awakening; and I, for one, think it's long overdue.'

'Thanks, Turner. I appreciate it. It was nothing against you personally, you know, but we had to be sure what had actually happened. This was a wake-up call about my brother, too. We're going to have to make some changes going forward. But that's what it's all about, isn't it? Change?'

Turner saluted her and turned back to his crew.

'What was all that about?' Connie said, coming up behind her.

'An apology, if you can believe it! I think Turner's had a bit of a comeuppance today. Maybe it'll serve him well in the future.'

Just then, a beaming Damon Powell came up, Marilyn on his arm. 'We're going to do it!' he announced.

'What are you going to do?' Gail said.

'We're going to tie the knot, as soon as possible. Hal thought he'd had a heart attack that night, but it turns out he's fine, just needs a little rest and recuperation. As soon as he's able, he's going to walk Marilyn down that aisle. We've decided there's no point in waiting any longer.'

'I think that's a grand idea!' said Charles. 'Are we invited?'

'Oh yes, you're all invited,' Marilyn said, eyes shining. 'We owe you all so much. We want you there to share our joy.'

'We'll be there,' Gail said. 'I can't think of any better way to celebrate our victory, can you, Connie?' She looked at him, eyes shining.

'No better way at all, my dear,' he said. 'Unless ...'

But she kissed him then, and the rest of his thought was left for another time.

We do hope that you have enjoyed
reading this large print book.

Did you know that all of our titles
are available for purchase?

We publish a wide range of high
quality large print books including:
Romances, Mysteries, Classics
General Fiction
Non Fiction and Westerns

Special interest titles available in
large print are:
The Little Oxford Dictionary
Music Book, Song Book
Hymn Book, Service Book

Also available from us courtesy of
Oxford University Press:
Young Readers' Dictionary
(large print edition)
Young Readers' Thesaurus
(large print edition)

For further information or a free
brochure, please contact us at:
Ulverscroft Large Print Books Ltd.,
The Green, Bradgate Road, Anstey,
Leicester, LE7 7FU, England.
Tel: (00 44) 0116 236 4325
Fax: (00 44) 0116 234 0205

DEATH WARRIORS

Denis Hughes

When geologist and big game hunter Rex Brandon sets off into the African jungle to prospect for a rare mineral, he is prepared for danger — two previous expeditions on the same mission mysteriously disappeared, never to return. But Brandon little realises what horrors his own safari will be exposed to . . . He must deal with the treachery and desertion of his own men, hunt a gorilla gone rogue, and most terrifyingly of all, face an attack by ghostly warriors in the Valley of Devils . . .

PHANTOM HOLLOW

Gerald Verner

When Tony Frost and his colleague Jack Denton arrive for a holiday at Monk's Lodge, an ancient cottage deep in the Somerset countryside, they are immediately warned off by the local villagers and a message scrawled in crimson across a windowpane: 'THERE IS DANGER. GO WHILE YOU CAN!' Tony invites his friend, the famous dramatist and criminologist Trevor Lowe, to come and help — but the investigation takes a sinister turn when the dead body of a missing estate agent is found behind a locked door in the cottage . . .

THE DEVIL IN HER

Norman Firth

The Devil In Her sees Doctor Alan Carter returning to England to stay with an old friend, Colonel Merton, after seven arduous years abroad — only to receive a terrible shock. He first encounters frightened locals who tell him tales of a ghostly woman in filmy white roaming the moors and slaughtering animals. Dismissing their warnings, he proceeds to Merton Lodge — and into a maze of mystery and death. While in *She Vamped a Strangler*, private detective Rodney Granger investigates a case of robbery and murder in the upper echelons of society.

FURY DRIVES BY NIGHT

Denis Hughes

Captain Guy Conway of the British Secret Intelligence sets out to investigate Fortune Cay, a three-hundred-year-old cottage on the Yorkshire coast. The current owner is being terrorised by his new neighbour, who Guy fears could be his arch-nemesis, an international mercenary and war criminal whom he thought he had killed towards the end of the Second World War. En route to the cottage, Conway rescues an unconscious woman from her crashed car — only to find that their lives are inextricably linked as they fight to cheat death . . .